D0560729

BAD TIMING

Also by Alan Scholefield

Burn Out
Buried Treasure

BAD TIMING

Alan Scholefield

HEADLINE

First published in 1997
by HEADLINE BOOK PUBLISHING

10 9 8 7 6 5 4 3 2 1

British Library Cataloguing in Publication Data

Scholefield, Alan
Bad timing
1.Detective and mystery stories
I.Title
823[F]

ISBN 0 7472 1145 0

Typeset by
Letterpart Limited, Reigate, Surrey

Printed and bound in Great Britain by
Mackays of Chatham PLC, Chatham, Kent

HEADLINE BOOK PUBLISHING
A division of Hodder Headline PLC
338 Euston Road
London NW1 3BH

My thanks for his help go,
as usual, to Dr Robin Ilbert,
formerly of the Prison Service.

Any mistakes are my own.

1

First the knocking. Then the unlocking.

It came into his consciousness, as it did every single early morning. It woke him. Sometimes it wove itself into dreams. It was distant knocking, right down at the end of B Wing.

Knock . . . knock . . .

It wasn't the kind of knock that says: May I come in? It was the kind of knock that says: *Wake up, you bastards!*

Then the rattle of the long key chain. It made a kind of tinkling noise in the echoing stone-built prison. And after the rattle came the sudden crash of the big key in the metal lock of the door, then the creak of the door being pushed open and the voice saying, 'Good morning!'

Ivor Taplin knew that this was what it was saying even though at the moment the voice was too far away for him to hear the words clearly. He knew because the voice would soon be saying, 'Good morning!' at his own cell door.

Like the knock, this pleasantry had its subtext too. It

was really saying: *Get up, you bastards!*

This whole process was called 'unlocking'.

He listened now as the chains and the keys and the voices came nearer. He lay on the bottom bunk; Ronnie was on the top. And Ronnie was still asleep. If his blanket was up over his head as it sometimes was, then the screw would come into the cell to see if he had died in the night. A death had occurred more than a year before when Taplin had been sharing a cell with someone else. This prisoner's brother had smuggled him some heroin. He'd been off it for nearly six months so when he gave himself what had been his usual shot he'd died of respiratory failure. Taplin hadn't known nor had the screw until he'd uncovered a corpse.

The other reason the screws would come in to look would be to see if the shape under the blanket was a dummy made of pillows, which would have meant that Ronnie Payne had somehow managed to saw through the cell bars and climb down the face of the prison then cross the exercise yard with its covering of anti-helicopter cables, then scale the perimeter wall and then slide down that and get into a car – or just run like hell.

Ronnie wasn't the sort of lad to do a thing like that. All Ronnie wanted to do was serve his time and get the hell out of there.

The screw was getting nearer and Taplin didn't want him in the cell. He pushed hard on the bottom of Ronnie's mattress which loomed above him, and went on pushing and jabbing until Ronnie's voice said, 'Yeah? What?'

'Unlocking,' Taplin said.

2

'Oh, Christ.' Ronnie thrashed about for a moment, stretched, then leaned over the side of his bunk and said, 'I was dreaming. I was fishing in the lake . . . you know, the one on the Winchester road? And I got into this carp . . . must have been five or six pounds . . . rod bendin' and me hangin' on, then the reel jammin' and me effin' and blindin' and—'

Knock . . . knock . . .

This time it was their door. The screw was in his dark blue uniform. He looked carefully at the two men. 'Good morning,' he said. They did not reply but even if they had he would hardly have heard them, for by that time he was moving to the next door.

'You want to go first?' Taplin said, nodding at the basin and the lavatory.

Ronnie leaned further over and Taplin saw his face with its white acne scars. 'Listen, let me tell you about this fish . . . Anyway, the reel unjams – and this thing goes streakin' off and takes nearly all the effin' line . . .'

'Ronnie, you want to go first?'

'I'm trying to tell you something. I'm— Oh, I get it. I know why you don't want to listen. You're going to see Doc Vernon today. That's it! You don't want to listen because you're thinkin' what you'd like to do to her. Am I right or am I right?'

Taplin slid out of his bunk and urinated. At first he had found it difficult to complete his bodily functions in company, but now, after serving more than two years of a four-year sentence, it no longer bothered him. He began to wash. Ronnie's voice went on. He was talking again about the fish he'd caught in his dream. Ronnie liked talking about his dreams, or if not dreams then his 'great exploits' as Taplin had categorised them, and usually he didn't mind listening; it helped to fill this small time capsule before the next time capsule – the fetching of their breakfast – arrived.

First the unlocking, then 'association', which meant washing and breakfast, and then the day would really begin. And today was an important day. Today – as Ronnie had said – he was seeing *her*. Doc Vernon. Sometimes he liked to think of her as Anne. The 'Doc' made it a bit formal.

He carefully dried his bit of soap and put it in a small plastic bag. Only two more days to go now of this routine, then he'd be washing in his own bathroom. Forty-eight hours. Ninety-six half-hours. A hundred and ninety-two quarter-hours. Two thousand eight hundred and eighty minutes . . .

He suddenly remembered a verse he had written on the flyleaf of a book when he was a twelve-year-old schoolboy and term was coming to an end:

> *This time next week where shall I be?*
> *Out of the gates of mis-er-eee!*

For the past month he had been counting the days and the hours. Nothing . . . *nothing* . . . must be allowed to go wrong. He thought of her body, white, small-breasted. He thought of her body every day now.

In the early days of his imprisonment he had also thought of it, but then his inner eye had seen it covered in blood. He didn't think of that part now.

2

First the knocking. Then the tea.

The knocking woke Anne Vernon that morning just as it woke her most mornings, except it wasn't so much a knocking as a mixture of hard sounds. Bang! That was the bedroom door in her father's part of the house. Crash! That was his bathroom door slamming. Woosh! That was his loo. All of this to an *obbligato* of BBC news from a radio in what he called 'a central position' i.e. a place he could simply put it down and where he could hear it from his bedroom, his bathroom, and the kitchen they shared on the ground floor, and where, of course, it disturbed the entire house.

Then a different noise: Creak . . . groan! Creak . . . groan! This was the tea coming up the creaking staircase in the hands of Watch. Knock . . . Knock . . . Then Watch's voice saying: 'Tea!'

He put it down on the bedside table then went to open the curtains. Anne had the sheet partially over her face and now opened one eye. Watch came into view. His slender figure was backlit by the morning sun, then he stepped out of the light towards the door and she saw him more clearly. His thin black face, topped by greying hair, wore its usual prim look. He was dressed in what was now his daily uniform: khaki trousers and a white shirt, bought for him by her father when Watch had come to live with them. He had arrived from Lesotho in southern Africa several months before, wearing a purple-and-gold tracksuit and her father had instantly bought him several less eye-catching ensembles.

'What time is it?' she said.

'Half-past six o'clock.'

'Oh God, why is tea so early?'

'It's important day for—'

'Watch!' Henry Vernon's voice came up the stairs. 'Have you seen my bloody tie?'

'Comin', Judge.'

She heard him going off down the stairs, then he stopped and called to her, 'Blekfas' half an hour.'

She called back quickly, 'I don't want anything cooked!' A small voice from the adjoining room shouted, 'I don't want anything cooked either.'

This was the last member of the Vernon household, Anne's daughter Hilly. Both knew that if they didn't get their refusals in first they might be faced with – well, anything . . . chops, steak, sausages, kidneys, bacon, eggs . . . separately or together.

Why was it always like this, Anne wondered. Why were her mornings like waking up in the Somme just after the battle had started?

The point was, it had always been like this even when she was a child in Africa in places like Lesotho and Nyasaland, when her father had been a peripatetic law

officer in the Colonial Service travelling from the courthouse of one little town to the courthouse of the next.
He had ended up a judge – still travelling the dusty
circuit – and Anne had been partially brought up in the
back of his truck and in one of his tents after her
mother, unable to stand the life, had bolted back to
Europe. And she had been brought up as much by Watch
as by her father. For Watch – her father's former legal
clerk, valet, right and left hands, and friend – was a man
who looked after people. 'Not because he has to,' her
father often said, 'but because he wants to.'

And the strange thing was that after joining his old
boss in the south of England some months before,
Watch had succeeded in changing at least this part of the
ancient cathedral city of Kingstown into a part of Africa
with which she was familiar. Take the tea, for instance.
She could smell it as it steamed away on her table. This
was not like any tea drunk in England; this was a brick
red liquid which smelled of iron filings and which she
would soon pour down the basin in her bathroom; just
as in Lesotho, when they were on their travels, she would
open the tent flap and pour the tea onto the hot dry
veld. Later, at her boarding school in England, she
tasted proper tea for the first time and found it was a
different liquid and that she liked it.

But the tea wasn't the only thing that was reminiscent
of Africa. Now, in summer, Watch would go round the
house closing the curtains against a tropical English sun
as he had done in their houses in Africa. Anne would
come back from work on a lovely sunny evening and find
the house in gloomy darkness with the lights on. Watch

had not got used to the fact that sunshine didn't mean Africa. She had thought of complaining but didn't like to upset him, for she had to admit that since her father had relinquished his position of housekeeper and Watch had resumed running their domestic affairs, things had certainly improved.

Although he had never been a 'servant' in Africa in the domestic sense – he had been more of a major domo – he had known from deep experience what constituted a well-run establishment and he had now put his know-ledge into practice. Meals were on time, the house was neat, and Hilly, who had greeted his arrival with suspicion, now treated him as Anne had treated him when she was Hilly's age – as a much-loved, if sometimes irritating uncle.

There was one other major African feature about the house: it smelled of polish in the way their houses out there had. Watch clearly loved the smell and had polished all the African artefacts her father had brought back with him; the Zulu assegais and the Bushman bows and arrows, the dried calabashes from Pondoland, the wooden stools from the Okavango. They were all set out now on walls and on the floor, instead of being in a jumble in her father's basement flat. Watch had polished all the furniture capable of being polished and eyed, with lust, the fridge and the dishwasher. Anne had had to dissuade him from giving them a waxy shine.

Today for the first time he was doing the school run with Hilly, and – of course! That's what his unfinished sentence had meant. He had said, 'It's important day for—' before being interrupted by her father who couldn't find his tie. She remembered now, it was the day Henry was going to see a legal firm about a job. What he described with heavy humour as, 'The next phase of my career.'

His retirement from the Colonial Service had not gone well. He had bought a cottage at the Cape of Good Hope, then became ill and Watch had phoned Anne in England. She had flown out to South Africa, brought her father back with her and now he wore a pacemaker and was relatively fine. But the illness and the move to Britain had broken the long partnership between Henry and Watch, and Watch went back to Lesotho to live with his sister.

Henry improved and, with Anne, bought a Georgian house in Kingstown. He became what he called, with deep contempt, a 'househusband', and cooked horrible meals for Anne and Hilly, did the school run, and even helped Anne in some of the investigations brought on by her work as a prison doctor. Then it was Watch's turn to find himself with problems. His sister and her new lover began to drain him of his British pension and he found himself supporting their entire family. So he had fled to England and now shared Henry Vernon's flat and did what he always did best: looked after them.

When her father had first heard about Watch's problems he had told Anne he was going to invite him over. She had thought this meant a two-week holiday, and it was only later she realised it was for something much more. She had been apprehensive to say the least. Fond as she was of Watch she foresaw for him a bleak future of loneliness, and an inability to settle in Kingstown.

What was she going to do with him? How was he going to be entertained? Who would his friends be? What indeed would he do all day?

These worries were now things of the past. Once he had decided to take over 'his family' again, life settled down into much the same pattern as she remembered from her childhood. Henry's family was his family, their friends were his friends, and his relationship with Hilly was the same as Henry's – grandfatherly.

She had also worried, in her more pessimistic moments, that Watch would be the subject, if not of violent racial attacks, at least of racialism. This too was unfounded. Kingstown did not have a large mixed population. There were a few Hong Kong Chinese, and some Indians and Pakistanis – all of these mostly in the catering trade – but few others. So Watch had a kind of curiosity value, especially as his face was intelligent and rather grave. At the library, of which he was now an active member, he was often consulted by the librarians about points from books on Africa. There, at least, he became a minor celebrity.

Because he was more adept at running a house than Henry he had naturally taken over. This meant that Henry had less and less to do. Retirement hung heavy. His temper, not always docile, became worse. He argued with Anne and Hilly and Watch and they all argued with him. Recently he had joined the Kingstown Club and had taken to going there for a game of billiards. He hated billiards but, as he told Anne, it was something to do. There he met a solicitor, also retired, who had worked in Kenya. They shared an African experience and met occasionally for a drink. When Henry expressed a desire to work again, the solicitor had said he'd write to a local firm and get him an interview on the 'old boy' network. The interview was today.

Anne stretched luxuriously in bed for a moment then got up and went into Hilly's room to give her a good morning kiss.

'I wish Watch wouldn't bring me tea,' Hilly said. 'I don't like it.'

'There are people in Africa who can't get up without a cup of strong tea.'

'But we're not in Africa.'

'Sometimes I wonder.'

She looked down at the small six-year-old and thought: My God, she's growing fast. Soon she'll be a teenager and then married and gone and I'll be a grandmother. She had to remind herself that this would not happen all at once.

Hilly said, 'Grandfather gets louder and louder in the mornings.'

'I know, darling. We'll get ear plugs. I'm going into the bathroom first. OK?'

She showered and towelled herself and inspected her body in the steamy wall mirror. She saw a woman with long legs and squarish shoulders and a waist that had at last gone back to where it was before Hilly was born. Her bottom was slightly larger and rounder and softer than it had been when she was playing a lot of tennis and her breasts were slightly heavier. But all in all she felt she still had things to offer. But to whom? There had been a man called Clive but that was all over now, and it had never been love, not in any real sense. Not a bit like the feeling she had had for Hilly's father, Paul. That had been real love and you knew what real love was like when you were carrying someone's baby and they brought that someone into casualty after a crane had fallen on him. Especially when you were the casualty duty doctor. Yes, you really did.

She brushed her teeth and then her short black hair and began to do her face. The good thing was she was living in the past less and less these days, not thinking of Paul as much as she had. She wondered for the hundredth time whether this was time healing the wounds or whether the memories were being masked by Tom's presence. Tom Melville was her boss and their relationship – or lack of it – was becoming complicated. She was aware that the lack of something couldn't really make it complicated, but she knew what she meant. As she dressed, she found that Tom's image remained with her. 'Come on,' she said to herself. 'Don't be so bloody silly.'

'Blekfas'!' Watch's authoritarian voice came up the stairs.

'Coming!'

Henry was already seated at the large kitchen table eating sausage, bacon and eggs. He was a man of medium height but looked shorter, for he was powerfully built. He was often dressed eccentrically in khaki Bombay bloomers and old tennis shoes, at which time he displayed a pair of muscular legs. Now he was dressed in an alpaca jacket and a white shirt with a black and white polka-dot bow tie. He was almost completely bald; what hair remained was white, and in the centre of his round

12

and ruddy face was a small white moustache.

'I heard you shouting about not wanting food,' he said into his sausage. 'Bloody ridiculous. You've a whole morning to go before lunch.'

'Good morning. That's how we usually start.'

'Good morning. There you are. Goodness, you're touchy.'

'Grandpa didn't say good morning to me either,' Hilly said. She was sitting as far away from Henry as she could get.

'Chatter . . . chatter . . .' he said.

'It's one of those mornings, is it?' Anne said.

She made herself some coffee and put a slice of bread in the toaster.

'You're teaching Hilly bad habits,' Henry said. 'What's this muck called she's eating? Fuseli? Well, it isn't good enough for a growing girl.'

'It's called muesli and it's not supposed to be enough for a growing girl. At school she gets a snack at morning break and then lunch.'

'Nothing's as good as home-cooked food.'

She could have pointed out that his own essay into the role of chef had proved disastrous, but didn't. Instead she took her breakfast into the living room and stood for a while at the window, sipping the coffee and nibbling the toast, and looking out at the beautiful street of terraced Georgian houses. Without her father's contributions, she would never have been able to afford to live in one. Before they had moved to Kingstown, she and Hilly had lived in London – and Anne had never considered moving out. Now, she thought, she would have to consider seriously before ever moving back.

As she had her breakfast she registered, not for the first time, that the living-room was shabby. When they had come to Kingstown they had spent so much on the house itself that there was nothing left for redecoration. Would she have to do it herself? She hated painting walls. This was a job she had briefly thought of for Watch when she worried that he would not have enough to do, but her father quickly disabused her of *that*.

'My God, when we moved into the cottage at the Cape, we painted the walls white. At least, that was the idea. Watch got so much paint on his face and hair that for days he looked like an albino. No, no, he is not a DIY person.'

As these thoughts were going through her head she was aware of a nagging conversation going on at the kitchen table. Hilly was saying, 'You shouldn't eat sausages. They're bad for you.'

Henry said, 'I've been eating them for years and they've never done me a jot of harm. Anyway, it's nothing to do with you what I eat.'

'You said I shouldn't eat muesli.'

'I'm your grandfather and I know about these things.'

Anne tried to block out the argument. She knew it wasn't a serious argument and that both were playing to each other, but it irritated her at this time in the morning and the play-acting was becoming more frequent as Hilly gained in sophistication. She often played the same mental games with Watch.

Hilly went on, 'It said on television that sausages were

bad for people. Sausages and bacon and fried things. Specially old people.'

Anne came back into the kitchen. 'Hilly! That's enough.'

'Is this how you instruct your daughter to address her betters?' Henry said with some indignation. 'She's an ageist.'

'What's ageist?' Hilly said.

'Oh, for God's sake eat your breakfast,' Anne said.

'But I only want to know what it is.'

'Enough!' Anne turned to Watch. 'You sure you know the way to Rangehurst?' This was Hilly's school.

Watch said, 'You told me three times. The judge he told me four times. I took the judge in the car yesterday. I know the way.'

'And you're dropping my father first, is that it?' Anne hadn't got into the habit of calling her father 'Judge'.

Henry said, 'Stop fussing.'

Anne said, 'I think I'll go to work. I know it's early but a prison seems a nice quiet place after this house.'

An hour later Watch drove Henry Vernon up Castle Street and dropped him in the centre of town. As he got out of the old 3.5 litre Rover on which he doted, he said to Watch, 'Looking for a job at my age is ridiculous.'

Watch said, 'It's your idea, Judge.'

'Of course it is. What the hell was I going to do to fill my time?' He went off into the King's Walk, a stocky, powerful man, and the early rush-hour crowds opened to let him through.

15

Watch then drove Hilly through the suburban streets to her school.

Hilly said, 'Have you got the letter?'

'Yes, I have the eh-letter.' He ran his tongue over his lips.

'Grandpa said he gave them your name anyway. And then Mummy wrote the letter.'

'I know that.'

'I just wanted you to be sure.' Then, as though to reassure him, she said, 'They're nice, the teachers. You'll see.'

Watch drove the large car with great care at not more than twenty miles an hour. 'We're going to be late,' Hilly said.

'We will get there.'

'Late.'

They reached Rangehurst in one of the leafy suburbs at exactly half-past eight. It had once been a large detached suburban house built at the end of the last century. It was on three floors and was cut off from the road by a high fence. The road outside the school was jammed with cars as mothers took their children inside.

'This way.' Hilly had Watch by the hand and led him through an open gate. 'You come this way in the afternoon too,' she said. 'They open it at three.'

'I know,' Watch said primly.

She led him into a small modern single-storey building which was a mixture of library and art room. Here there were four teachers representing the four classes in the school. 'This way.' Hilly tugged Watch towards one teacher already surrounded by children and mothers. A slight hush fell on the room as Watch became the focus of attention. Hilly bathed for a moment in the penumbra of his radiance. She pushed through the crowd to the teacher at the centre.

'Good morning, Hilary,' the teacher said.

'Hello, Miss Jennings. This is Mr Watchman. He's bringing me to school now.'

'Malopo,' Watch said.

For a split second Miss Jennings, a small and puckish young woman, thought this might be an arcane ethnic greeting and opened her mouth to say, 'Malopo,' but Watch anticipated her by saying, 'It is my name. Mr Malopo.'

'He's Mr Watchman Malopo,' Hilly said, tasting fame again.

'Oh, yes,' Miss Jennings said. 'Your grandfather gave us his name. But we asked for a letter saying he was going to bring you to school and pick you up.'

'Watch has a letter from my mother,' Hilly said.

Watch produced the letter and Miss Jennings read it and nodded. 'That's fine, Mr Malopo. Sorry to seem so severe, but it's school rules. Which part of Africa are you from, if I may ask?'

'Lesotho.'

'Ah . . . I'm not sure where that is exactly.'

Watch was used to this and gave his stock answer. 'It is an independent country in the middle of South Africa.'

'Oh, yes,' she said vaguely. Then, 'Right. Fine. Well, the bell's just about to go so I'll take Hilary now. And you'll be the one to come back here at three to pick her up, is that right?'

'I think so. But maybe her mother. Maybe her grand-father.'

'Oh dear, it's getting complicated. Anyway, I know you now. Come on, Hilary, we've a lot to do this morning.'

Miss Jennings, like the other teachers, moved slowly towards the door with her class around her like so many ducklings, and Watch and the mothers streamed out of the library towards their cars.

3

Kingstown is a cathedral city, but the cathedral itself is only one of three major buildings. On top of the hill overlooking the city lie the ruins of the ancient castle. The cathedral, which has been compared to Winchester, is in the centre of the city surrounded by its Trollopean close. Between these, halfway down the hill and partly hidden by high cypress trees, is the prison. It is a true Victorian house of correction and was built in the middle of the last century by the Birmingham architect D. S. Hill, who also built Lewes Prison. The front is made of flint and brick, and twin flat-topped towers flank the main gates. There are four wings built in the shape of a cross, and Tom Melville, the head of medicine at the prison, had said to Anne on her first day there, 'Can't you just see the Victorian ecclesiastical mind at work? The image of the Cross – redemption through punishment?'

But this cross, Anne had later realised, was surrounded by high walls, on the top of which were rolls of razor wire. It is an old prison and in spite of new additions – the hospital, for instance – it looks and smells old. On the north side it is still possible to see places where the screw handles protruded into the cells themselves. These machines were used as punishment. The prisoner turned the handle in the cell for a certain length of time and the warder in charge could tighten the screw from the far side of the wall to make the job harder and harder. The warders were now called screws and the prison itself was known to prisoners and discipline staff alike, even to the Governor, as the 'nick'.

Anne parked near the big main doors, locked her car carefully – being near a prison meant *more* danger from theft, not less – and went towards the entrance. When she had first arrived, the car park attendant had told her to knock and she'd be let in. The echoing noise made by her firm knocking had shaken her and she had never knocked loudly again. Now she entered the gatehouse.

''Morning, doc. 'Morning, doc. 'Morning, Doc . . .'

The voices came from all sides and she nodded and said a general, 'Good morning.' The gatehouse was always a busy place. It was filled with deliveries of food for the kitchen, lengths of wood for the maintenance staff, as well as office equipment, and bathroom and cleaning materials. Other prison gatehouses were not like this, Anne knew. They were modern. They had had money spent on them. All Kingstown Prison had were promises of money. There was talk of the prison being downgraded, there was even talk of it being closed. But then there had been talk like that for many years.

She had to pick her way towards the duty officer, whose office was up in one of the gatehouse walls.

''Morning, Doc,' he said from his seat behind bullet-proof glass, and dropped her keys down the wall funnel. She scooped them from the metal basin and went off towards the hospital.

She was still feeling jangled from breakfast and decided that before she did anything else she would make herself a strong cup of coffee. Her room was done out in pale green. Tom, who had planned it, had been rather proud that the first female doctor on the medical staff should have a room in a rather more sensitive colour than the creams and browns of the prison itself. Pale green wasn't Anne's favourite shade but she had no intention of changing it.

She had just poured herself a large mug of coffee when there was a short knock on her door and Tom Melville put his head round.

'Hi,' he said. 'Got a moment?'

'Coffee?'

He shook his head. 'Can't stop.' He was a tall man, now wearing a white coat. He was thin and angular with thick black hair in which there was an occasional glint of grey. He was in his late thirties, a few years older than Anne.

'I've got some news and I wondered if you'd have lunch?'

'Good news, I hope.'

'Excellent news.'

She suddenly had an uneasy feeling that he might have been promoted to a bigger job somewhere else and caught herself hoping he wasn't.

'Well, tell me.'

'Can't. I've got to see the Governor in a minute.'

She looked at her diary. 'And I've got to see a prisoner, but I'll be finished by lunchtime. Fine, I'd love to.'

'See you at the pub at twelve-thirty.'

Suddenly he was gone. That was a characteristic of Tom's. While he talked to you he was buzzing and fizzing with kinetic energy, hands moving, arms moving, then suddenly he stopped – and vanished.

She sipped the hot coffee, still uneasy about the 'excellent' news. The prison service was in its usual state of upheaval. There were now private prisons and they were pirating staff from places like Kingstown. It wouldn't surprise her at all to learn that Tom had been recruited by some private prison in the Midlands at a better salary. And if he went, would she stay? When she had first come she had thought of it only as a temporary job. She had taken it when a job in London fell through. By then she was a single mother looking after Hilly – and suddenly her father was ill. She had needed the money and the security. But now the psychiatric side had become more and more interesting. She wasn't a psychiatrist but, like Tom, she was expected to produce psychiatric reports on remand prisoners going for trial and on any other prisoner who was thought to need one. Anything serious would then go one step further to a Home Office psychiatrist for a more detailed report.

She put her head out of her door and called to her assistant Les Foley, 'Could you get me Ivor Taplin's medical record, please?'

Foley, a plump man with dimples and a motherly manner, came into view in the passageway. 'I got it out yesterday,' he said. 'Knew you'd want it.'

She took the file and went back into her room to study it.

The subject of the file had finished his breakfast. He had listened with waning attention to Ronnie Payne's breathless fishing dream, had taken his tray back to the servery and now sat in a hardbacked chair just outside his cell, waiting for a barber to come in from A Wing to cut his hair. He wanted to look good for Betty.

Would she notice? Would she care?

He daren't let himself think like that.

But it was difficult not to, for Betty was part of what was happening to him – and what would happen to him. He hastily changed his thought pattern and went over again the formal aspects of his release. He knew he would be asked questions and given advice by several men, by a Deputy Governor, by the chaplain, and by a security prison officer. There would also be a report from the medical officer. He began to think of Doc Vernon. He was seeing her later. He liked to think about her. She was the one caring person in an uncaring world. Not even the probation officer, who was supposed to, had shown that he gave a damn about what happened to Taplin.

He had seen him in his small office off C Wing the previous day. His name, which was on a little wooden plaque on his desk, was Bryan Coles. He was younger than Taplin and his black hair was wavy. He wore a striped shirt and rolled sleeves and a copper arthritis bracelet on his wrist.

'Come in, come in . . . take a seat.'

Taplin had, from day one, obeyed orders. He had made that decision while he was a remand prisoner awaiting trial. He had also decided on two other things: to plead guilty to the charge, and never, ever do anything that might increase his sentence. So he now sat on the straight chair in front of Coles's desk.

'Let's see, now . . . Taplin. Ivor Taplin. How old are you?'

'Forty-six.'

'Right. And your address?'

'Seventeen, Mulberry Street.'

'That's near the Cathedral, isn't it?'

'On the other side of it.'

'Right.' Coles leaned back in his chair. It was an elderly swivel chair. The upholstery had worn and some of the white stuffing was showing. 'Well, this is it, isn't it, Ivor?'

'Yes.'

Coles flicked a sheet of paper. 'You've served your time well. No added days. No loss of remission. So you've served two years out of four and it's time to go outside.' He flicked the paper again. 'You've no psychiatric history, so that means that even though you're on conditional release you're going to be pretty much on your own. You think you can deal with it?'

'Yes.'

'No problems?'

'Not that I know of.'

'Let's see. You were an estate agent, weren't you?'

'Yes.'

'But your company was taken over and you lost your job. When was it taken over?'

'Four years ago.'

'Did you get another job?'

Taplin could have said: 'What does it say in the report?' but didn't. That too was ingrained now. You didn't challenge people like Coles nor speak to them unless they spoke to you.

'No,' he said. 'I didn't.'

'So you were out of work for two years before . . . well, before it happened?'

'Yes.'

'Did you try to get a job?'

'Yes.'

'Are you going to try and get one now?'

'Yes.'

'OK. The point is, as I said, you're going to be pretty much on your own. Is your wife still in your house?'

'Yes.'

'Are you . . . I thought you might be divorced after what happened.'

'She's a Catholic.'

'Right. But I want you to remember, if your wife says . . . well, if she complains about you – I mean, if you do anything to her – then it's back here. You understand that, don't you?'

'Yes.'

'You understand that you're only on licence for two years – that you've not finished your sentence?'

'Yes.'

'For most of that time you'll have to report to a probation officer at the offices in Queen Street. You know where they are?'

'Yes.'

'I'll give you his name and telephone number, OK?'

The interview had gone on and on. Sometimes there had been new information, but mostly information had been repeated not once but twice, especially about how he was to live. The standards expected of him. After all, Coles said, he was an 'educated' man. As though that made any difference. His education hadn't kept him out of prison.

'You wanting a cut?' a voice said.

Taplin looked up and saw the barber from A Wing who was serving two years for fraud. He was small and dark and was carrying clippers and a sheet.

'That's right.'

'OK, I'll do you now.'

The King's Walk links the High Street of Kingstown with the Cathedral Close. It is a very old arcade with small staircases going up into the buildings that line it, and it reminded Henry Vernon, as he pushed his way through the morning crowds, of some of the wynds in Edinburgh off the Royal Mile. Like many old English commercial areas, the office numbering was eccentric and it took him some minutes to find number 23, on the door of which a brass plate said: *Bannister, Burleigh & Bleache, Solicitors at Law*.

He went up to the first floor and there the ancient aspect of the place gave way to more modern interior decoration, but only modern in the sense that the seventeenth century had given way to the nineteenth. Anyone born in the Victorian age would have approved entirely of the decor of Bannister, Burleigh & Bleache. It was dark with heavy wooden fittings and was the kind of place that Henry knew well. Most of the courtrooms in which he had worked in Africa had been designed by British architects of the early twentieth century, and were heavy with mahogany and local hardwoods which helped to make them blisteringly hot places in summer, and dark and gloomy places in winter. There had been a Dickensian air about some of them.

'Yes?' the receptionist said. 'May I help you?'

'My name's Vernon,' he said. 'I've got an appointment with Mr Baker.'

The woman looked down at the appointments book. She was in her forties, Henry guessed. She wore no make-up and had a pinched look about her small mouth. Large spectacles seemed to cover the entire upper part of her face. Her hair was caught back in a bun. She looked up at the long-case clock near the door and said, 'You're a little late.'

'Couldn't find the place. The numbering is medieval.'

An expression of irritated surprise crossed her face. 'Mr Baker is taking a call,' she said coldly. 'He won't be long. Please have a seat in the waiting room.'

The waiting room was also dark, and on this bright sunny morning the electric lights were on. Watch would have approved of this, Henry thought, as he settled himself into one of the armchairs. The walls were covered with glass-fronted bookcases packed with legal tomes. Henry felt a wave of nostalgia. He picked up *The Times* and glanced at the front page. At first he did no more than look at the headlines, expecting at any moment to be called by the receptionist.

Then he read page one, then went on into the body of the paper. He read . . . and he read . . . Half an hour passed. He got to his feet and marched back into the reception area. The receptionist did not look up.

He cleared his throat. She glanced at him and said, 'I'm afraid Mr Baker has had to take several calls. He'll be with you in a short while.'

'That's what you said the first time.'

She frowned. He could read in her expression that she considered him presumptuous.

Henry said, 'I know senior partners are always busy but he does know I'm here, doesn't he?'

'Yes, Mr Vernon, he knows you're here. And Mr Baker isn't a senior partner. He is not a partner at all. Mr Baker is the practice manager and—'

The buzzer went and the woman pushed down a small switch. A man's voice said, 'Miss Moberly, is the old chap still there?'

'Yes, Mr Baker.'

'Send him in then.'

Miss Moberly looked up at Henry and her pinched lips spread into a small smile. 'Mr Baker will see you now. First door on your right.'

Mr Baker was a thin intense-looking man in his thirties. His desk was covered in paper but all the papers were in neat piles. Henry imagined him spending a great deal of time sorting them into piles before doing anything about them. He did not get up or offer a hand but simply said, 'Take a seat.'

He picked up a letter. 'Says here you were doing

something in the law out in Africa.' Henry decided the letter must be from the solicitor at the club. 'Whereabouts?'

'Lesotho.'

'Where's that?'

'Southern Africa.'

'Anyway, what were you doing there?'

'I was a judge.'

If Henry had hoped to impress Baker he was mistaken. He simply said, 'And now you want to be a legal clerk, is that it?'

'A what?'

'Legal clerk – that's what it says in the letter. That's what I'm looking for. We've just lost one.'

'I thought . . . well – something in an advisory role.'

'Advising on what – African legal practice? You're retired, that's right, isn't it?'

'Yes.'

'Can't expect to be a senior counsel, can you?'

'No, of course not. It's just that . . . well . . .'

'Mr Vernon, we have an opening here for a legal clerk. If you're not interested then both of us are wasting our time.'

Henry's mind flicked briefly back to the house where all he did now was get in Watch's way, and the club where he played boring games of billiards through the long afternoons, and said, 'I'm interested if there is an interesting future.'

Baker ignored that. 'Says in the letter you can start any time.'

'That is so.'

'Come on then, I'll show you your room.'

'Now? Today?'

'Not today. Tomorrow. OK?'

'Yes, I suppose so.'

Henry's 'office' was in what had once been a corridor. The end of the corridor had been blocked off and an old desk had been shoved against the wall. There was also a photocopier, a guillotine for cutting paper, a filing cabinet, and a hatstand on which hung an old, broken golf umbrella.

'You play golf, Mr Vernon?'

'No. I used to play tennis in Africa.'

'They had tennis courts in . . . what was the place?'

'Lesotho. Yes, they had tennis courts. And golf courses. And swimming pools. And cricket pitches and rugby fie—'

But Mr Baker had turned away and was going back down the passage. 'See you at eight-thirty,' he said.

4

'Here's Taplin, Doc,' Les Foley said, at the door of Anne's room.

Taplin sat down in the chair opposite her. She thought he looked older than when she had last seen him, but that's what prison did to people. It put lines on their faces and grey in their hair. He was dressed in regulation blues, a man of medium height but on the slender side with a face she would have passed in a crowded street without a second glance. She didn't like Taplin but told herself that likes and dislikes weren't important; neutrality was all.

'Well, time's nearly up,' she said. When she had first come to the prison she had said to a prisoner about to leave, 'Looking forward to it?' and he had replied, 'Of course I'm fucking looking forward to it! What d'you think?' She had realised then that the angry reaction was more her fault than his. So she repeated what she now said to all prisoners coming up for release. 'Nervous?'

'A bit.'

'Have you seen the probation officer?'

'I saw Mr Coles. He's told me what the system is. I'm

on licence for two years and I've got to report to them for two-thirds of that time.'

She nodded. 'It'll go quickly.' She tried to make her voice less cold than it sounded to her. 'Did you get on all right?'

'I think so.'

'Right. Well, I've got to give you an examination to prove that you're physically fit for release. You haven't had any real problems since you came in, have you?'

'Just my stomach.'

'How is it now?'

'Not too good.'

'That's probably tension. I'm going to give you enough tablets for four or five days and I'll write a letter to your GP. But now I'll weigh you.' She did so and noted the figure. 'There's very little change, so you're not entitled to a new set of clothes.' She examined him quickly but methodically and made one or two notes. 'Right. You can put your shirt on.' Again, because her voice had sounded cold, she tried to be slightly more friendly and said, 'Is your wife coming to fetch you?'

'No. I told her not to. She doesn't like the nick.'

'I don't blame her.'

'Doc, can I say something?'

There was a momentary catch in his voice and she prayed he wasn't going to cry. She had had crying prisoners before and they made her feel helpless. Tom said they cried because she became for a short time a surrogate wife/lover/mother. She knew he was probably right but she'd been new then and didn't like the thought of being that kind of figure to most of the men in the nick, especially to people like Taplin who had been sentenced for a savage attack on his wife. She found it specially hard to remain neutral to wife-beaters and people who abused members of their families.

Now she said, 'Of course you can say something.'

'Can this be confidential?'

'That depends on what it is.'

'It's about my wife – or, I should say, about me and my wife.'

She held up a warning hand. 'Be careful what you say now, Taplin. We wear three hats as prison doctors. One is that we have a duty to protect the general public. Another is that we have to make court reports on prisoners for judges, and if they think we're neglecting to give all the information we have, they can come down on us pretty hard. But we do also have a relationship with our patients which is confidential. Do you understand that?'

Taplin was twisting his hands, those same hands, she knew, which he had used on his wife's face. She had seen him several times. She had done the initial court report and then she had seen him medically. She had had to force herself to be sympathetic on one occasion when she had sensed he wanted to talk to her, but he had finally withdrawn and she had been glad.

He was still looking down at his hands and she wanted to get the interview over so she said, 'Let me put it at its most basic. If you're going to tell me that when you leave here on licence you're going to harm your wife, then I've got to do something about it.'

He shook his head. 'No, I'm not going to harm her.

Oh, I know what you're thinking: here's a man who beat up his wife and now says he won't harm her. He would, wouldn't he? But that's what I want to explain. You've been good to me. You're the only person in the nick who's been good to me, and I want you to know why I did what I did.'

'All right, tell me, but just remember that if I feel what you're saying is potentially dangerous to anyone I've got to report it.'

'And you won't tell the probation people?'

'I told you – I won't tell anyone.'

Taplin paused, then said, 'Did you read the Judge's summing up in my case?'

'I must've. I don't recall the details.'

'You don't really know much about me, do you? But you know I lost my job, because I remember telling you.'

'Did you? I'm sorry, I must have forgotten. I've done scores of reports since I did yours.'

'Sure. Let me tell you then. I was an estate agent and my firm was taken over. There was what was called "restructuring". Four of us lost our jobs. They said I was bound to get another – but how do you get another when the housing market's in ruins? I wrote about three hundred letters and I got seven replies. Don't ring us, we'll ring you – that was the message. You want to know what humiliation is? *That's* humiliation. And in his summing up that's the reason the Judge gave for me doing what I did to Betty. He said I'd been humiliated. And I'd attacked my wife because she was the nearest thing to hand. But he said that thousands of people had lost their jobs and hadn't attacked their wives or anyone else.'

Now Anne began to hear a different kind of story from any she had heard before. He spoke in a flat unemotional voice, starting with his house which he described in detail because, she realised, that was what he had mostly done in life – described houses. Interested despite herself, she began to see the house he was talking about on the far side of the Cathedral. She knew the streets were narrow and old and winding up the hill, with rows of attractive terraced houses dating from the early part of the last century.

'We paid more than we should have, more than we could afford really, but everyone was wanting to get on the house ladder. If you didn't get on then you'd never get on. That's what people were thinking.'

'I remember.'

'We bought this terrace house and it became every-thing to us. I've thought about what happened a lot and I see it meant almost the same thing to both of us. We didn't have any kids and the house became specially important to us. For Betty it was social cachet and for me, well, it showed my success.'

They had to pay a heavy mortgage but they were both working and this was the bustling eighties and the housing business was booming. He was doing well. Then came the recession. The take-over of Taplin's firm and the recession occurred just about the same time, and then the bottom fell out of the housing market.

They both panicked when he lost his job. How were they going to pay the mortgage? Betty Taplin had worked in the cosmetic department of a big Kingstown store and she started, in her spare time, selling beauty products from door to door. She would come home from the store when it closed and pick up a heavy bag and go out to the Kingstown suburbs and in summer would not be back until nine or ten.

Taplin said, 'She'd never sold anything before except behind a shop counter but she started doing quite well. Then she began to give selling parties. You know what they are?'

'I think so,' Anne said.

'You invite friends and friends of friends and give them tea or a drink and then you show them the stuff and they buy it – you hope. Well, they did. There must be something about Betty because the parties were a success and she started selling more and more on her rounds and pretty soon she had to give up her job at the store. Eventually she was making more money in a week than I ever made at the height of the boom in the housing market.'

'So she was the breadwinner?'

'That's what happened.'

He had become what Anne's father, Henry, had called a househusband and what others called a 'new' man. But it seemed to Taplin that most men chose to become new men. He hadn't. He wrote letters applying for jobs and he did the shopping with the money Betty left him and he did odd jobs around the house. He repapered some rooms and painted others and he fixed anything that was broken. He became a handyman.

During this time, Betty was working fourteen-hour days and often did not get home until late. She would eat her supper which he had made and kept hot for her, and then she would drop into bed.

She began to drink. They'd never drunk much before. Taplin would have a couple of beers watching sport on TV and Betty might have a gin before lunch on Sundays. But now she began to drink at the selling parties and continued into the weekends.

'It usually started with a selling party on a Friday night,' he said. 'I knew she was drinking then because I used to serve the drinks and the food. I assumed it was because she was nervous. She'd go to bed a bit drunk, pleased she'd sold something. But after a few months she started having a hair-of-the-dog on Saturday mornings and that became drinks at lunchtime and she stayed pretty much drunk the whole weekend. And that's when the problems really began.'

At first the problems had been arguments and rows. Why hadn't he done this? Why hadn't he done that? How much had he spent on the shopping? Where was the change? Where was the supermarket receipt for her to check?

But the bad question was always, *When are you going to get a job?*

By Sunday the liquor had made her surly and aggressive. One day she attacked him physically. At first he had thought it was an accident. He had walked from the living room into the kitchen and had been hit in the face by a broom handle. He had thought that somehow the broom had been resting against the door and that it had fallen as he went through. But then she had screamed at him and hit him again.

'I made a grab for her,' he said to Anne, 'but I couldn't

hold her. She was like a mad thing. She's only tiny, not more than five-two and doesn't weigh much, but I couldn't hold her. She was in a kind of frenzy and that gave her strength. I managed to get the broom out of her hands and then she started scratching and biting. I don't know how long it went on, probably just a few minutes, then suddenly she stopped. She seemed to collapse, as though she was made of rags. I thought she was dead at first so I carried her into the bedroom and put her on the bed. She was unconscious and she slept from the middle of that Sunday afternoon until early Monday morning. And when she woke she asked me how I'd got the marks on my face.'

He'd thought that this was just a moment of madness brought on first by his work troubles and then the amount of time and energy she was putting into hers. So he said nothing. But it didn't stop. It always happened at weekends and always after she had been drinking. She would begin to pace around the house and a sense of foreboding would come over him that something horrible was going to happen. Then suddenly she would attack him.

He said to Anne, 'A man will attack with his fists. There's something natural about that, but she attacked me with anything that came to hand.'

She hit him in the chest with an iron, she tried to stab him with a kitchen knife, she threw plates and fruit and the toaster at him. She hit him on the knee with a heavy frying pan.

He pulled out his shirt and undid his trousers, and above the top of his underpants Anne could see on his belly a broad mottled scar. 'I was asleep,' he said. 'She burned me with a gas poker.'

'Did you tell anyone? The police? The social services? Your doctor?'

He shook his head. 'I kept on thinking I would, but then when it came to the point I couldn't.'

'Why not?'

'Because I loved her. Strange that, isn't it? I mean, she was doing me harm yet I loved her. I kept on thinking that when she went berserk she wasn't Betty any longer but someone else. I used to look at her when she slept. She always seemed like a child. You couldn't imagine her doing what she'd done.'

'But telling someone might have helped. You mightn't have become violent yourself.'

He thought about that for a moment and nodded. 'The Judge had it right about humiliation.'

'But he was talking about you losing your job.'

'And he was right about that. That was bad enough. You wouldn't know because you've probably never lost a job – and anyway, you're not a man. Men are supposed to have jobs. We're supposed to be the breadwinners. And when we're not, we're humiliated. I had to learn to live with that. But that's nothing to the humiliation of being beaten up by your wife. I suppose that's really why I didn't tell anyone.'

'So you just lived with it?'

'I had to.'

But then a day came when the humiliation reached its worst moment. Betty had gone out shopping one Saturday morning and Taplin had made a casserole for lunch.

In cooking it, some of the gravy had overflowed onto the cooker top and the house was smelling strongly of burnt food when Betty came back. He knew she had had a couple of drinks before going out and he thought she had probably stopped in at the nearest pub for a couple more.

She flew into a rage about his carelessness and said she wasn't going to eat burnt food. He offered her a spoonful of it to taste, saying that it wasn't the casserole that had burned but just a little gravy on the stove top. She smacked the spoon out of his hand. He said nothing, served himself and sat down to eat.

'She came up behind me and pushed my head down. I tried to struggle out of her grip but I told you in these moods she was very powerful. She pushed my face down until it was in my own food and held it there for a few seconds. Then I managed to throw her off.'

'I'd warned her that I was going to smack her face if she went on attacking me. Well, until then I hadn't. It was just a threat. Now I did. I held her against the wall with my left arm and smacked her face with my right hand. I don't think it was a hard smack. It wasn't meant to be. But something came over me then because I couldn't stop. The next thing I knew was that I had her on the floor and was using my fists and . . . and there was blood all over the place.'

'What then?'

'I didn't know what to do. She was unconscious. So I dialled nine-nine-nine and the police and the ambulance came round and I was arrested and she was taken to Kingstown General.'

'I looked this up in your papers a few minutes ago. Mrs Taplin was pretty badly hurt, wasn't she? I mean, more than lacerations and contusions. There was nerve damage too.'

He looked down at his hands again. 'I'd crushed her left cheekbone.'

'And her teeth were badly smashed.'

'She lost three in the front.'

'I should think that's why you got a heavy sentence. The Judge must have been sympathetic to your wife. She'd been very pretty, hadn't she?'

'Very.'

'And you never told your lawyers about being battered by her?'

'I just couldn't. Apart from anything else, I was feeling desperate about what I'd done to her and I needed to atone. That's what I tell myself anyway. But it was, I suppose, fear of more humiliation.'

'I can understand that.'

'So . . . that's it. That's what I wanted to tell you. I pleaded guilty so I didn't have to tell anyone why. But I wanted you to know.'

'I'm glad you told me.'

'And it won't go any further?'

'No, it won't. And good luck.'

5

'Sorry I'm late,' Anne said.

Tom Melville was standing in the saloon bar of the King's Arms nursing a low-alcohol lager. The pub was in one of the narrow cobbled streets that ran down into the town from the castle. When they had first begun to go there, Tom had described it as 'a proper pub – no music, no Formica, no one-armed bandits'. There were scrubbed pine tables, red velvet curtains, and the place smelled richly of ale. In winter there was a cheerful fire. As far as Anne and Tom were concerned, its major attraction was that it was a little too far from the prison to draw other staff. He bought her a spritzer and they took their drinks onto the terrace and sat under the plane trees.

'I had to see Taplin,' Anne said.

'Who?'

'Assaulted his wife quite badly.'

'Do I know him?'

'Estate agent.'

'Oh yes, I do remember him vaguely. I saw him once in surgery.'

'He goes out tomorrow and I was seeing him for his report. He made me feel rather bad. I've disliked him ever since I first saw him. And now it turns out that he thinks I like him and that I'm . . . well, that I've been good to him.'

Tom laughed. 'I told you that you were just a mother to them.'

'It's embarrassing, specially as he gave me a background to his behaviour which put a completely different slant on things.' She reported briefly what Taplin had told her.

'A battered husband! Well, that's interesting. I had one once and did a little research. There are a hell of a lot more of them around than we know. I came across the figure of one-in-three.'

'Battered?' She could hardly believe it.

'Well, perhaps not battered. But in a survey, one in three women admitted to having attacked their husbands at some time.'

'This was the real thing, apparently.'

'He could have been lying.'

'He struck me as telling the truth. I think I'm getting better at judging that, these days. And I've read a bit about battered spouses. There wouldn't have been much point in lying to me. The time for telling that story was to his solicitors so it could have been heard in court. But he just pleaded guilty then. He didn't want anyone to know that he was being battered. I believe him. Pride. It went on for months, apparently. She even burned him. Finally he snapped and lost all control. Anyway . . . that's why I'm late. We had a long talk.'

'I'm just glad you could make it.' He pulled out a letter from his pocket and tapped it. 'From Steffie,' he said. 'She's gone to live in France.'

'Stephanie's gone?' She could hardly believe it.

'Went over yesterday, apparently. Isn't that great?'

'God, you must be relieved.'

Stephanie was Tom's ex-wife, a woman Anne had met several times and whom she could not stand. She remembered how elegantly she dressed. Thinking of her now she saw in her mind's eye a slender woman with black hair, dressed in black trousers and a white polo-neck sweater. Not long after Anne had started work at the prison, the gatehouse officer had buzzed her surgery and said, 'There's a Mrs Melville to see you.'

'To see me? You must mean Dr Melville. He's in London today.'

'No, she said you, Doctor.'

'What does she want?'

'She hasn't said. She's a bit . . . nervy, if you know what I mean.'

She had put a mac over her white coat and run across the open space to the main gate.

'She's in the shelter, Doc,' one of the prison officers said. 'Wouldn't come in.'

The building was like a large bus shelter opposite the main gates in which visitors could wait out of the rain. Over her white polo and black trousers Stephanie was wearing a black trench-coat flung casually over her shoulders. In the grey light her face had looked drawn, almost haggard.

'How can I help you?' Anne said.

There were deep shadows under her eyes but the eyes themselves seemed to blaze like an animal's. She was smoking and now ground out her cigarette under a stiletto-heeled pump.

'I'm afraid Tom's gone to London,' Anne went on, still thinking she must be wanting him. Stephanie lit another cigarette. There was something unsettling about her whole demeanour.

Suddenly she said, 'Why are you doing this?'

'Doing what?'

'Don't pretend. You know what I mean.'

Anne was confused. 'Look, is there anything I can do to—'

'Please do not patronise me!' Stephanie had begun to pace up and down. 'Do you think I do not know what is going on?'

'Is there something going on?'

'Between you and Tom.'

Anne gave a small laugh. 'I'm afraid you've made a mistake.'

'Don't lie to me. You think you can hide behind a child? You think I don't know what goes on?'

'Mrs Melville, I really can't stand here arguing with you about something like this. There's nothing between Tom and me. Nothing at all. Whether you believe that or not is up to you, but I don't want you coming here and accusing me, or Tom for that matter, of something that isn't true.'

Stephanie had walked away a few paces and then turned to stare at her. 'Tom is no good for you. He can never love someone like you. This is a warning, you

46

understand. Next time, things will be different.'

Nothing had been going on between them then nor, indeed, the next time Stephanie had made contact with her – although that time it was only her voice on the telephone that had come between them.

Tom had invited Anne and Hilly to the Welsh Marches to spend a weekend at his mother's home. Anne had been put in Tom's old room and late at night, when she was already in bed, he had brought her in a malt whisky. They had chatted and he had kissed her. She had been half-expecting that. If you allowed a man into your bedroom late at night with a bottle of whisky in his hand, there was no way you could tell yourself that what happened next was all an enormous surprise. Until then, because Tom was her boss, she had told herself that what was happening must never happen. But telling and doing were different. However, just at that very moment, the telephone had rung at her bedside: it was Stephanie. Tom had taken it. Hilly was asleep in the room next to Anne and she was woken by the ringing. By the time Anne had returned from reassuring her and getting her back to sleep, Tom had vanished. After that, there had been lunches and the odd dinner in Kingstown, but that was all.

Stephanie had made other calls to Anne, and threats of suicide to Tom, and one serious attempt to harm herself. But now, at last, things were changing. Anne said, 'You mean leaving permanently or just going on holiday?'

He opened the letter and read: ' "*I am first going to*

47

have a holiday, perhaps a week in Paris, then I am going to look for properties in the Var. They say there is a lot of money to be made by letting nowadays. I will live in the house in Port Grimaud . . ."'

'That was her father's holiday house,' Tom said. 'We went there several times.'

'Where's she getting the money to buy properties?'

'Her father left her quite well off. And I'm paying her something.'

'Well, that sounds permanent,' Anne said. 'You can't run properties in France and live in England.'

'That's what I'm praying for. Just to have the Channel between us will be something.' He swirled the drink in his glass. 'And it'll make other differences, too. It'll give me a feeling of freedom, of release, that I haven't had since the divorce. There were always her threats of suicide. Sometimes she meant them, sometimes it was bluff.'

'It was simply blackmail.'

'Yes, of course it was. The real problem was that I could never tell which was which.'

'The divorce was her idea, wasn't it?'

'She thought she'd snared a merchant banker, but he was too shrewd to be used and when that went wrong and he dumped her, she wanted to come home. But there was no home to come back to, and we were divorced. Who knows, she may find another merchant banker and marry him this time. God, I wish she would. When I think of the money I'm sending her each month – money she doesn't need – I could weep.'

'What a waste.'

'I wouldn't mind so much if I could get my own life together.'

Here it was; the tightrope. She had sensed that something important was coming, otherwise why meet in the King's Arms on an ordinary working lunchtime? Suddenly she didn't want to hear what he had stored up to tell her. Just being with him sometimes made her tense and uncomfortable. There was always so much left unsaid between them. Stephanie had been one reason, but the other was what had always bothered her: the fact that he was her boss. How do you have an affair with your boss? She knew that every second secretary was supposed to be doing that, but they didn't have a complex home-life as she did. Often she would think how marvellous it would be to leave it for a weekend with Tom, and go somewhere no one would know them, somewhere she could be totally anonymous for a time.

She felt he was waiting for her to comment on how he was proposing to get his life in order, but instead she finished her drink and said, 'She always made me nervous.'

He opened his mouth and closed it. She thought for a moment he was going to say something more, but then he finished his own drink and said, 'What about something to eat?'

She said, 'I'd better get back, I've got Taplin's report to write.'

'Look, this needs celebrating. I mean properly. What about dinner?'

She hesitated only for a moment. 'I'd love that.'

49

'You get a feel?' Ronnie Payne sniggered. 'Doc Vernon give you a feel?'

Taplin came into the cell carrying his lunch tray. Payne was already at the small table they shared, wolfing down cannelloni and chips.

'No, she didn't.' Taplin sat down and began to pick at a salad. He was too nervous to eat much.

'I done it with a doctor once,' Payne said. 'In her surgery. My own doctor went away on holiday and this woman doctor is there lookin' after things for him. They got a name for it . . .'

'Locum.'

'Nah, don't think so – something else. Anyway, I goes to see her. I got this sore leg, and she says, "Take your jeans off" and I take them off and she comes at me. I mean, I know the score. I been come at before. So I oblige her, right there on the couch where she sees patients. I mean, I give her a hell of a good time and—'

'Ronnie is this another dream?'

'What you saying – that I'm having you on? I swear I'm telling you what happened. And beautiful, I mean really something!'

'That sounds like one of your great exploits.'

'You're bloody right, mate.' He put some chips on a slice of bread and stuffed it into his mouth. As he chewed he watched Taplin pick at his salad. Then he said, 'What you doing when you leave here? Going home?'

'Why?'

'You think your wife wants you there after what you done to her?'

'It's my house.'

'You better watch yourself, mate, that's all the advice I can give you.'

'I will.'

'You can't never trust a woman. I mean, I know women and I'm telling you, you can't trust 'em.'

'I'll remember that.'

'Yeah, you remember.' He looked at the dessert. 'Bloody prunes and custard. You think they could do better than that.'

'I quite like prunes.'

'Quaite laike . . . Christ! Listen, why'd you think your wife's going to welcome you home? I wouldn't. I read about it in the papers. She nearly lost an eye, didn't she?'

Taplin went on with his salad.

'And she never came to see you much.'

'I told her not to. I don't like her coming to a place like this.'

'How old is she?'

'Round about my age.'

'You ain't got kids, have you?'

Taplin shook his head.

'That's what women want. Kids. Your wife want kids?'

'Perhaps.'

'Why not have them then?'

Taplin didn't answer.

Payne put down his dessert spoon with a bang. 'You know something? We been together in this bloody hole for nearly three months and I don't know nothing about you. But you know everything about me, even my dreams. I tell you those because I want you to know.'

'And your great exploits.'

'Yeah, and my . . . listen.' His face puckered in uncertainty. 'You having me on? Because if you are—'

'But that's what they are,' Taplin said. 'Great exploits. My God, I wish I'd done some of them. I mean, coming second in the Monte Carlo Rally. That's really something, a really great exploit.'

'Yeah.' Payne looked uncertain again, as though he had some difficulty in remembering this motoring success. 'Yeah, I done well.'

He took his tray back to the servery and returned to lie on his bunk. He said, 'I want you to do something for me.'

Taplin said, 'If I can.'

'I want you to go to Winchester. See my old mother. I'll give you the address. Tell her I'm doing my bird good, that I'll be back to look after her. Tell her I'm going to get a job and we'll buy a cottage. Ask her not to worry. You know something? She brought me up as straight as a die. She didn't want me to be no criminal. And I'm telling you something else, Mr Ivor Bloody Taplin. I should be leaving before you! I should be getting out before you. Fair's fair.'

It always came down to this. There were the dreams, and the pathological lies, which Taplin had categorised as the 'great exploits' to differentiate them from the dreams. But somehow, dreaming or lying, Ronnie Payne always managed to bring the conversation round to what he considered was the great injustice of his life, that Ivor Taplin was being released on licence and he wasn't.

Taplin didn't want to argue any more. Instead he said, 'I'll tell your mother you're doing well.'

'Yeah, you do that. I'll give you the address.'

Taplin already had the address, but he wasn't going anywhere near Winchester. That was his own bit of lying.

6

'We're having a Watchman roast,' Hilly said.

'That's nice,' Anne said, kissing her daughter on top of her head.

It was early evening and Hilly was sitting at the big kitchen table watching a portable TV which was on one of the shelves. Whenever Hilly was in the kitchen the TV set was on. She seemed, most of the time, not to be looking at it but any suggestion that it be turned off drew protest. But often when Anne returned from work, she was not in the mood for whatever soap was showing and switched it off. She did so now.

'MUMMY!'

'Sorry, but I've had people talking at me all day and I want a calmer atmosphere.'

Watch, who was at the stove, checking the vegetables, said, 'TV gives indigestion.'

'Only if you eat the TV set,' Hilly said.

'Very funny.' Anne peered over Watch's shoulder and said, 'Those carrots look gorgeous.' They were being finished in butter. 'Can I have one?'

Watch moved slightly to one side allowing her to get

55

her fingers on one. His body language showed that he disapproved.

'Lovely.'

Watch had known how to cook before he worked for Henry, but during their long legal life together had done little. It was Watch who hired the cooks. When Henry retired and they lived in the cottage at the Cape of Good Hope, he took up cooking again and gave Henry all his favourites. These were relatively simple. He liked roasts – Hilly had nicknamed them 'Watchman roasts' – with a variety of vegetables. If not roasts then he would make do with smoked haddock and poached eggs. This menu had expanded under pressure from Anne and Hilly, although Henry could never see any reason for having anything else.

Now Anne said to Watch, 'I'll have to take a rain check on the roast. I'm having dinner out tonight, but I'll have some cold tomorrow.'

'Who are you having dinner with?' Hilly said.

'Tom Melville invited me.'

'When are we going to his house again? I want to see Beanie.'

Beanie was a diminutive dachshund to whom Hilly and Anne had lost their hearts.

'Why can't we have a dog?'

'Because there's no one to look after it and that wouldn't be fair on the dog.'

'Watch is here.'

Watch cleared his throat and his body language grew more specific. Everything about it said NO.

'Where's Grandpa?'

'Downstairs in his flat.'

Her father was usually one of the group in the kitchen when she got home, enjoying a whisky and soda and encouraging Watch in his culinary endeavours. She turned to Watch and said, 'Is he all right?'

'The Judge is eh-tired.'

Anne went to the top of the stairs and called down to Henry's sitting room: 'Father?'

'Here.'

'You all right?'

'Yes, thank you.'

'Don't you want a drink?'

'I'll come up.'

He *was* looking tired, she thought. At first she wondered if he might be ill, but he accepted a whisky and soda and sat near Hilly at the end of the big kitchen table.

'Well, how did it go?' Anne said.

'How did what go?'

'Your interview, of course.'

'Oh, that. I have employment.'

'That's marvellous.'

'Yes.'

'When do you start?'

'Tomorrow.'

'That's sudden, isn't it?'

'They're short-staffed.'

'And what'll you be doing?'

'There's plenty to do.'

'Are you going to court?'

'They've described the job as advisory. I think that about sums it up.'

'So you'll be giving opinions. That won't be much different from when you were a judge. I'm delighted. You must be too.'

'Rather.' It came out flatly.

'Did you go to the club this afternoon?'

'Just for an hour or two.'

She told herself he had probably had a couple of drinks to celebrate, which was why he looked tired.

Hilly said, 'Miss Jennings had an accident.'

'Who's Miss Jennings?' Henry asked.

'You know Miss Jennings. She's my form teacher.'

'Oh, that Miss Jennings.'

'What happened?' Anne asked.

'She was riding her bike at lunchtime. Going down to the shops. And she got hit by a car and now she's got a broken something.'

'Oh dear.'

'And there was a mess this afternoon at pick-up time. Ask Watch.'

Anne turned to Watch. He shrugged. 'It was not much.'

'It *was* much,' Hilly said. 'They wouldn't let Watch take me. I told them who he was and I told them Miss Jennings had a letter from you and I told them I *knew* him and that he lived with us and they *still* didn't want to let him take me, and they had to go and find the letter in Miss Jennings's filing cabinet and then they found it and they let me go!' She came to the triumphant end of the sentence and drew a deep breath. 'And now they're going to get a new teacher until Miss Jennings can come back!'

58

'Well, that's very exciting but I'm sorry for Miss Jennings,' Anne said. 'Is she in hospital?'

'I don't know. If she is, will you take me to see her?'

'If I've got time and if she is in hospital.'

'How will we find out?'

Henry said, 'You ask. They tell you.' He turned to Anne. 'She doesn't seem to learn much, does she?'

Hilly said, 'I won at Scrabble when we played yesterday.'

'Only because you cheated,' her grandfather said. 'Whoever heard of a word like *ool*?'

Anne and Tom had been to La Venezia several times. It had opened the year before and was not the typical Italian restaurant of the English provinces. There were no bunches of straw-covered *caraffinos* hanging from the ceiling and no bunches of artificial fruit and vegetables. It was cool and elegant, and sometimes Anne rather wished it was more in the 'British' style of Italian restaurants. The ones she had gone to with Paul had always been those with bunches of things, and she loved them. But she had to admit that the food in La Venezia was very good and the welcome was just as friendly.

'Ah, dottore,' the head waiter said to Tom as they went in. 'Please. Here by the window.'

'He always remembers you,' Anne said after they were seated.

'Well, we've been here a few times. Now this is a celebration, so let's celebrate. What about a *punt e mes* to start with while we look at the menu?' The drinks arrived and he held up his glass. 'Here's to Stephanie – and may she stay in France for the rest of her life and never come back into mine.'

They drank, then he said, 'I phoned my mother this afternoon to tell her the good news. She's put up with quite a lot from Steffie too, having to cope with her visits after we were divorced. Steffie went on treating her like her mother-in-law. She would ring up and ask to come and stay. Sometimes she just pitched up and Mother was too kind-hearted to tell her to get lost.'

They had *antipasto* then he ordered liver and Anne veal with lemon and they had a bottle of Barolo.

'Do you think she'll stay in France?' Anne said.

'God knows. She always said she wanted to live there even when we were married. You know I met her when I was in Africa working for a medical team in one of the drought areas and she was working for a charity? Well, she hated the place. Couldn't stand the locals. Blamed them for the drought. Blamed them for dying of starvation. Before she went she'd thought of Africa as an extension of Europe. But I think I was too smitten to take this in at the time. It only dawned on me later. Coffee here or at my place?'

It was said without pause for breath. Anne had in a sense been waiting for a moment like this and she said, 'Here, I think.'

'Right.' His voice was expressionless. He ordered two espressos. 'Would you like a *grappa*?' She shook her head. 'Nor me . . . Listen, that was just an invitation to coffee, you know. It wasn't loaded. It wasn't a come up and see my etchings.'

'Yes, it was.'

He laughed. 'Well, yes, I suppose it was.' Then he said, 'It's just that we don't seem to be lucky. Or at least I don't – I mean, about getting you to look at my etchings.' He paused and then said intensely, 'And I really very badly want you to come and look at my etchings. That's the Barolo speaking but it's a fact.'

She nodded. 'Well, if we're going to let the Barolo do the talking then let it say on my behalf that I don't want to come and see your etchings here. I mean in Kingstown.'

'Can I ask why not?'

'Because . . . well, I'll put it as simply as I can. You think that because Stephanie goes back to France you're released from a great encumbrance and you can start a different sort of life.'

'Precisely.'

'But that doesn't apply to me. My reaction is very simple and it has nothing to do with Stephanie; it has to do with you. You're my boss and one doesn't go looking at one's boss's etchings.'

'Good God, I'm not that sort of boss! I mean, the one you're constructing. I don't arrange my life that way.'

'I know you don't. But I still see you as my boss with all that that implies.'

'Aren't you being a bit old-fashioned?'

'That may be one way of putting it, but it doesn't change the nature of responsibility. Just say we became lovers off-duty but something went wrong at the prison – I did something which I shouldn't do, or didn't do something I should have done . . . how would you react?'

'I hope in a civilised way. However, the whole thing is academic since it hasn't arisen.'

'But it easily could. And if you did your duty you'd come down on me quite hard. You'd have to, because the Governor might be expecting you to. The point is, I don't think I could be made love to by you one minute and be scolded by you the next.'

He held up his hand. 'Thank goodness we've dropped the etching metaphor. But listen, this is important to me. Or what I should say is *you're* important to me. You must know how I feel about you and you—' She opened her mouth but he said, 'Let me finish this before the Barolo wears off. I want to be with you not just during the course of the professional day, but off-duty as well. I want to live with you. That's what I'm saying.'

It was now her turn to laugh softly and he looked offended. She reached out and covered his hand with hers. 'Don't be upset, I was just thinking about my off-duty life and your off-duty life. You have a miniature dachshund to worry about. I have a small daughter. A father. And a kind of African relative. How do you propose that we live together?'

He nodded slowly. 'Yes, I can see the complexities. But didn't you say that your father and . . .?'

'Watch.'

'I always think of him as "Clock". Anyway, didn't you say that your father and Watch had lived together in Africa after they retired? Why couldn't that be arranged again? Most people have families. But they don't all move in together when their children find mates.'

'You make it sound easy, but—'

'There are ways. But that's not what I'm talking about right now. I'm talking about us. You and me. If we want to do something we can arrange things. It's the wanting to I'm on about. Look, the most important person in all this is Hilly. I know that. She comes first. She needs a father. I know you think that too. Little girls of Hilly's age need fathers. All I'm doing is putting in for the job. There are perks, of course. You're the perk.'

'That a very nice thing to say and you're right about Hilly. But, my God, you'd be loading your plate with worry.'

'Don't you understand? I want to worry about someone other than Steffie – and that's a different sort of worry.'

'Is there any more of that wine left?'

'Just a little.'

'That's all I want.' She drank and then said, 'I've got an alternative. And this really is the wine talking. In a situation like this I believe in going slowly. So this is what I suggest. Let us, you and me, go away somewhere neither of us have been before; somewhere no one knows us and where you won't be even the shadow of a medical chief of staff. And let's take it from there.'

He turned her hand and gripped it with his own. 'When?'

'As soon as we can.'

'I'll drink to that.'

63

7

Ivor Taplin walked down to the end of the prison driveway and turned left onto the Royal Avenue. This was a road which wound down the hill from the castle, straightened out as it reached the prison and then dropped down into the city. In the twelfth century it had been built to connect the river ford to the outer bailey of the castle, and was said to have been the road on which Richard I travelled when he came back to England after the Third Crusade.

There was a bus stop directly outside the prison but Taplin decided he would walk. He was carrying a black nylon shoulder bag and was dressed in sports jacket and trousers and a blue shirt, the clothes in which he had come to prison. Doc Vernon was right, he thought. His weight hadn't changed and so the prison didn't owe him new clothing. He thought of her in her office and how she had listened to what he had to say. This was the one decent memory of his last days, almost the only decent memory of the last two years.

He walked down the hill tasting the air, feeling the early sun on his shoulders, seeing the clouds coming slowly in from the south-west. Everything seemed new.

It was still too early for the morning rush hour. When he stopped at a bakery and bought two bacon turnovers, he wondered if he looked like a discharged prisoner, but the girl who served him hardly glanced at him. He ate while he walked. He couldn't ever remember anything as tasty. He thought of the breakfast being dished up in the servery. He wasn't going to miss that, not ever.

Ronnie Payne would be getting his breakfast now. His breakfasts had made Taplin feel physically ill. He'd mix things. He'd put bread and butter and jam with his porridge or eggs or both. He'd sometimes want sandwiches filled with chips. He always ate pasta with chips.

Thinking of Payne brought the whole feeling of prison back to him, its smells and its sounds, and he knew that something would always do that. There would always be a trigger; for the rest of his life, there would be moments when he would suddenly go plunging back.

That morning Payne had been more than usually aggressive and provocative. It wasn't surprising. He had another six months to go on two charges and was always whining about why Taplin was going out and he, Ronnie, was staying. It seemed to do no good explaining that these were his second and third burglary offences.

'Yes, but I never hurt nobody,' he always said in reply.

It had happened again that morning. Taplin had hardly slept and was up and dressed at five. As soon as Payne had woken, he started bitching about his remission.

'I've told you a thousand times,' Taplin said. 'It isn't remission. Well, not like you think of it, anyway. It's not for good behaviour or anything. It's because if you're sentenced to four years and you behave yourself, then the law says you can be freed on licence when you've served two.'

'Why can't I be freed on licence then?'

'Anyway, you'll get a third off.'

'Listen, let me tell you something. Nobody's going to treat Ronnie Payne like that. I'll see the Governor. I seen him once before, when I was in last time. He says to me then I'm a model prisoner but he daren't let me out because burglary is what's bothering everyone these days.'

Taplin said mildly, 'Let me give you some advice, Ronnie. The next person who shares your cell isn't going to be like me. You tell these whoppers to him and you'll get done. It'll be right round the nick.'

'What you saying? You think I'm lying?'

'I've said what I think, and it's for your own good.'

Payne had come sliding down off his bunk and had stood in front of him.

'You take that back! You ain't going to leave this place if you say things like that. Me lying! Listen . . . I was a black belt in karate. Two chops – wham! wham! – and you're done, mate! Done!'

Taplin looked at the pathetic figure with the thin, acne-scarred face standing in the middle of the cell. The thought of Payne being a black belt at anything – even burglary – was laughable, but Taplin didn't want trouble, especially on this day. He simply said, 'All right, Ronnie. I was only having you on.'

That was the last time he had seen Payne, because

after unlocking the formalities of his release were begun: the return of his belongings, the brief interview with a senior manager who told him that he didn't want to see him back in prison. And then out into the street. For a moment he had glanced at the area where relatives waited but Betty wasn't there. He was glad; he hadn't wanted her to be there and had written to tell her so.

He finished eating his bacon turnover and turned away from the High Street, crossed the Cathedral Close, and went into a network of narrow streets, some of which could trace their origins to medieval times. Mulberry Street was one of these, although the houses were no older than the early nineteenth century. They were small and pretty. Some houses were pink-washed, some white. Doors were mainly yellow or black. Number 17 had a black door. He stood outside it. He had thought of it for so long and in such detail that to see it once again brought a lump to his throat.

He unlocked the door and went in. There was a musty smell that comes when the windows are kept shut. He knew the smell of old. 'Betty!' he called.

There was no reply.

The curtains were partly drawn and the house, on this bright morning, was gloomy. He stood in the sitting room. There was the sofa, the two matching chairs. He had thought of the chintz coverings many times but now saw that he had not got them quite right. There was more red in the flowers than he had realised.

'Betty!'

It was early. She should still be at home. She should be at home anyway on this day. He went to the window and looked for her car but he couldn't see it.

He went up the stairs to the two bedrooms and the bathroom which formed the top floor. Would she still be in bed? Is that how she was waiting for him? He had thought of her in such intimate detail – and was it now coming true?

The bedroom, their bedroom, was empty, not empty of Betty – that too – but empty of everything he remembered. It was a sitting room now. There were chairs, a table, and a small sofa. He walked over to what had been the spare room. There was a single bed in it and a small dressing-table with Betty's cosmetics on it. He went into the bathroom. Yes, there was her shower cap and her towel. He stood there for a minute or two then went downstairs again. He crossed the small passage and opened the dining-room door. The table and chairs were gone. There was a single bed here too, a small table, an armchair and a chest of drawers and wardrobe. On the bed was a clean towel. Against one wall were his books, his old tennis racquet, a couple of dozen long-playing records, his stereo system, a box containing his CDs and tapes and there was also a TV set. The room was crowded with his possessions to the point that he could hardly move in it.

He sat down on his – yes, it must be his – bed and stared blankly at the wall.

Was this how it was going to be? Was this what she would do?

What, he asked himself, had he expected?

Well, more than this.

The point about Betty was that he had loved her, and

she him. That's what she had said many times, right from that very first time when he had taken her out for a picnic on the Downs and they had made love on a rug in the sunshine. He had considered himself a lucky person, not only having Betty but having the house and a job that was bringing them in a decent salary. And then . . . and then it had all gone sour.

But even then he had loved her.

He admitted to himself now that she had not often come to see him in prison. In the early days he had felt at his worst about what had happened. Later, in his second year, he had realised that if both of them made an effort they could save their marriage. Later still he had stopped thinking about saving his marriage; he was just thinking about her as she once was and how he would court her and chat her up – chat up his own wife. Crazy, but wonderful.

He got up off the bed, went into the sitting room, and began to pace. His mind seemed to be turning very slowly. He knew that something fundamental had happened within the house and therefore within Betty's mind, but what exactly it was he had no idea.

He went out into the street again and began walking aimlessly.

'Payne,' Anne said, looking down at the file in front of her. 'Ronald.'

'That's me.'

'So what can I do for you? Are you ill? Is something the matter? You should have seen Dr Melville at surgery.'

'It's you I want to see, Doc.'

He was sitting across the desk from her in her light-green room. The sun was hidden by cloud and on this summer morning the green gave the room a chilly feel.

'All right, you made your appointment and you're seeing me. Can you tell me what it's about?'

'I want to talk.'

'What about?'

'Well, things . . .'

Sometimes prisoners chose to see the doctors instead of the security staff to tell them of rumours of unrest. Some months before, a man had come to Anne and told her there was talk of a riot. He had named names. The men in question had been split up, some being sent to a different prison, and no riot had broken out. These were called security information reports – SIRs – and might even take the form of notes dropped on the desk of a prison officer or a brief word with a member of the security staff.

Anne wondered what might be forthcoming from Payne. 'What things?' she asked.

'Things about me.'

She pulled a pad towards her and said, 'All right. Tell me.'

'I want to tell you why I done it.'

'Did what?'

'You know what.'

'You don't have to tell me. Didn't you tell the Judge?'

'I got to tell you and maybe you can help.'

'Help how?'

'You know how.'

71

'I'm afraid I don't, Payne.'

'Well, you haven't heard yet. You see, I done the burglaries for a reason. I was starving, see. My mother as well. We needed bread.'

'But the Social Security Department would have seen to that. They would have given you income support or something else.'

'Social Security? They never done nothing for us! They said so. They said: "Ronnie Payne, you're a bad boy and you get nothing from us".'

She decided to humour him. 'Bad boy? What did they mean by that?'

'Previous form.'

'Oh, yes.' She glanced at his file. 'You went down for burglary twice before, didn't you?'

'Yeah. We was starving then too. My father was a millionaire, you know. But he never gave us a penny. Wouldn't marry my mother. Oh no, not good enough!'

'What exactly is it you want from me?'

'I want you to put in a word for me like you done for Taplin.'

'I don't follow you.'

'You put a word in for him, otherwise how's he got his sentence reduced? I mean, it stands to reason. Here's a bloke that duffs up his wife and he gets four years and he's out in two. You got to ask yourself how's that. I says to him, "Taplin, how the hell you get away with it like this? What you been telling Doc Vernon?" And he says he's been telling you the truth. "I told her the truth, Ronnie." That's what he says. So now *I'm* telling you the truth.'

'But I can't help you in getting your sentence reduced, you must know that.'

'But all I done was thieve a little. I didn't hurt nobody. And the insurance pays. That's what I'm saying to you. I got to sit out my sentence in this prison because I burgled when I was starving and did it for my old mum.'

Anne tapped the file. 'It says here that you have no parents alive. That your mother died some years ago.'

He ignored her. 'Listen to what I'm saying. I got to sit out my sentence but Taplin is in for GBH and he gets away with half.'

'As long as you don't make trouble you'll get remission.'

'Yeah, but you don't see? I only done burglary and I'll be here for two years. He done GBH and is here for the same. Now is that fair?'

'It's your third conviction, Payne. That makes the difference. It was his first for grievous bodily harm.'

'Yeah, but—'

'I just can't help you.'

'But—'

'You'll come up for parole like anyone else, and as long as you've behaved yourself you'll get it. So you may not even serve two-thirds.'

'Yeah, but—'

'I'm sorry, but I must stop it there. If you think you've been unjustly treated, why don't you see one of the Board of Visitors' members, and if he thinks you have, he'll make representations to the Home Office.'

'Hey, that's good. I could do that, couldn't I? They got clout, ain't they?'

'I don't know how much clout, but they certainly take things seriously. If you've got a case then that's the route. All right?'

He rose. 'Yeah.' Then suddenly he stopped and his thin white face puckered into a frown. 'But you never sent Taplin to see these people. Why you want me to go?'

'It's your third offence, Payne.'

'Oh, yeah. That ain't good, is it?'

'No, not very.'

8

Ivor Taplin walked slowly down the High Street. Once it had been choked by cars but since it had been turned into a pedestrian precinct, it was now clear of smog. He had, in his time, sold several properties in the High Street. That had been in the early eighties when things were taking off. Now there were several shops with boarded fronts. Kingstown hadn't recovered fully yet from the recession. Nor, for that matter, had he.

He felt in a kind of limbo. There were no rigid rules to govern his behaviour now as there had been the day before, and he wasn't sure yet exactly how to behave. He had wandered up to the parole office but at the last moment decided not to go in. The same feeling had overtaken him when he had found himself outside the Social Security office. He just didn't feel like registering in such places on his first day of freedom. He would do that tomorrow.

He spent several hours wandering the streets. Once a policeman had looked at him and he had frozen inside. He had realised he must look like a vagrant. Not in dress, for he was dressed well enough. No, he realised that in his walk, and in his attitude, he was displaying all the signs of aimlessness that vagrants displayed.

He quickened his step and gave it a purposefulness that he did not possess. Should he go home? But the empty house with its rearranged rooms depressed him. In fact, the whole aspect of the day depressed him. He knew in one part of his mind that prison was much worse, that seeing Payne eating one more breakfast would have driven him up the wall, yet the prison day was ordered. It had, if not purpose, then enough checks and balances to occupy his time. And there were always the time capsules themselves: association, work, meals, library, TV, the exercise yard, the gym, lock-up, lights out. They may not have been much in themselves, and he may have hated them individually and together, but what they did was order his life – and in a way he missed it.

He found himself down by the river. It ran through the lower part of the city and was said to hold trout. He had no interest in fishing, but wondered if he should take it up. The water was owned by the city so fishing was not expensive. It would give him something to do if he couldn't get a job. And if he couldn't get a job before he went to prison he didn't give himself much chance now.

But what would Betty say? Thinking of her, he wondered again where she was.

He assumed she was out on her rounds selling cosmetics. But where? Which part of the city? If he knew, he would have taken a bus and searched for her.

Or would he?

Was she trying to tell him something by not being

there? Or was she just being practical? Money had to be earned; money was needed. Maybe she thought he would only get out of prison later in the day. Maybe he had not told her he would be arriving before breakfast.

He knew these thoughts were nonsense. The house was changed. The rooms were changed. There was no double bed any longer. That was the difference.

But wasn't it natural? He'd been away for two years. Wouldn't most women have done what Betty had done? Wasn't it just a method of giving them time to get used to each other once more?

He felt a burning sensation coming up from his stomach and took one of the pills Doc Vernon had given him. Would the doctor have reorganised her house if her partner had gone to prison? Did she have a partner? He knew she wasn't married because he'd heard someone in prison mention it. There was always talk about Doc Vernon as there would have been in any all-male prison. One thing he knew was that he would never – could never – have hit *her*, no matter what she'd done.

He tried to put her out of his mind but couldn't. Someone in the prison said she had a little kid. He liked that idea. That's what had gone wrong between Betty and himself. Two years of being locked away with his thoughts had made him believe in that simple answer. If they had had a kid, none of this would have happened. He'd been tested. His sperm count was on the low side – but all right. She'd had her tubes blown. But they'd never achieved anything.

He'd never told Doc Vernon that side of it. Perhaps he

should've. Perhaps . . . Everything was perhaps. Perhaps if they'd had a kid . . .

He saw a phone box come up and on impulse he stopped and looked at the phone book. Vernell, Vernham . . . here it was. Vernon, Dr A Vernon – then the address in Castle Street. He knew Castle Street well, had sold a couple of houses there over the years. He wondered if this was one of them. He wasn't far from Castle Street, he could go and check; it would pass the time until Betty got home.

The street was as he remembered it, on a slope with rows of terraced houses facing each other. Each house was a carbon copy of the next and he couldn't remember which ones he'd sold. There were trees in the street and one was opposite Doc Vernon's house. He stopped in its shade and looked at the house. It seemed rather run down. The paint was peeling from the downstairs window frames and flaking on the front door. Even so it was a nice house and he envied the people who lived in the street. A feeling of bitterness passed over him. He had had a terrible experience but the people in this street probably just went on with their lives. Why had it happened to him?

Noticing a bench in the shade he sat down. There was only one doorbell on the house, which meant that it had not been split up into flats. So she owned it all. Doctors must be paid bloody well in the prison service to have a house like this. Maybe she did private consultations as well. Had to be something like that.

The afternoon air was warm and the street was quiet. He began to doze. He wasn't sure how long his eyes had been shut but he was woken by a car pulling up opposite him. A small girl and a black man got out. The black man opened the house door and the two of them went in. He frowned. No one in the nick had ever mentioned anything about a black man.

He was still pondering this when he saw a thick-set man with white hair, wearing an alpaca jacket and a bow tie come walking down the street and enter the house. That must be Doc Vernon's father. He'd heard about him but hadn't known he lived in the same house – or at least he assumed he lived there because he'd used a key.

And then Doc Vernon arrived in her small car. He knew what make it was, he even knew its colour and year of manufacture. It was one of the many things he knew about Doc Vernon.

The whole family was in now, plus one man he couldn't identify. He wondered what they would be doing. Laughing, joking, telling each other about their day? He rose and walked slowly up the street until he found a supermarket, where he bought two steaks. Betty liked steaks. He made his way to Mulberry Street.

When Anne entered the kitchen, Watch was reading the paper and Hilly was sitting at the table watching TV. She started to move in the direction of the TV to switch it off, then decided to put up with it.

'Hi, everybody.' She unloaded her shopping onto the table, kissed Hilly and lifted the lid of a casserole on the stove. 'That looks good,' she said to watch.

'It is eh-not cooked yet,' he said, and she knew that what he was really saying was, 'Don't taste.' So she didn't.

'We got a new teacher today,' Hilly said. 'Miss Garth.'

'Oh? Why?'

'Because Miss Jennings can't come back this term. She has got a broken hip. No, not broken. Another word. Disconnected.'

'Dislocated.'

'They said it was disconnected.'

'All right, disconnected.'

'And she has to stay in hospital with her leg in a tractor.'

'I think that's probably traction.'

'No, it isn't. That's what they said.'

'OK.'

'So Miss Garth is going to teach us.'

'How old is she?'

'Ancient. She was at the school before I went but retired because she was ancient.'

'Did you like her?'

'She's deaf.'

'Yes, but did you like her?'

'She's all right. We only have her till the end of term and then next term Miss Jennings comes back.'

'Where's your grandfather? Isn't he home yet?'

'He's downstairs.'

She frowned. This was the second time. 'Is he all right, Watch?'

'He says he's tired. I say he is not a young person. Why is he working? He doesn't need to work.'

'It gives him something to do.'

'He was telling me he was writing a book about the law of the old days.' This was true. Henry had been

80

writing on the English medieval legal system, something
that had always interested him with its parallels to some
of Africa's social structures. 'Why he give this up?'

'You've got a point. I'll ask him.'

She went down into her father's flat. It too was now
neat as a pin and smelling of wax polish. It had two
bedrooms, one of which Watch used. 'Father?'

He did not reply and she went to his back door and
saw his figure in the garden. She went out to him. He
had changed into more comfortable clothes – torn khaki
shorts, old and disreputable tennis shoes that had been
white many years before, and a frayed safari jacket – and
was lying back in a garden chair.

'Tired?' she said, as she pulled one up next to him.

'A little. I think I'm not used to work. Got out of the
habit. I'll get used to it again.'

'But do you think you need to?'

'What, work?'

'Well . . . get used to it again?'

'Why ever not?'

'You don't need to financially, and unless you enjoy it
you—'

'Of course I enjoy it! What on earth are you suggesting?'

'Not a thing. It's just that you were writing a book and
now you're not.'

'Oh, that. Who would want to publish that?'

'That's not what you said when you started it.'

'Yes, but who would?'

'There are legal publishing houses. Any one of them
might be interested.'

'I doubt it.'

They sat in the late-afternoon sunshine for a few moments without talking and then she said, 'You'd tell me if you weren't feeling all right?' He did not reply and she went on, 'It would be foolish not to.'

'I'm feeling fine.'

'I think Watch is worried about you.'

'Watch worries too much. Look, I want to work. I can't just sit around the house. And the book I can see now was just something I dreamed up to fill in time. This is what happens when you get older. Work is what keeps you young.'

'If it's interesting work I suppose it does.'

'Well, the law *is* interesting. I had to give an opinion today.'

'Oh? What about?'

'It's too complicated to explain.'

Hilly's voice shouted from the kitchen window, 'Mummy! Phone!'

'Who is it?'

'Tom Melville.'

She went up to the phone in her bedroom.

'Hi,' Tom's voice said. 'I'm ringing about what we discussed. Places to go to.'

She had been waiting with some unease for this moment and said, 'Yes?'

'You said places where we weren't known.'

'Right.'

'Do you know Bath?'

'Never been there.'

'I have once, when I was a teenager. Does that count?'

'No, that doesn't count.'

'Well, listen, I've got to go there next week. There's a meeting at one of those conference hotels just outside the city. I can get away from it on Friday at lunchtime. What about if we met in Bath and had a good lunch and took it from there?'

She paused. It was Hilly's last day of school. She said, 'And stay where?'

'I've looked up some places and we can talk about them later. I just wanted to know whether in principle you thought this was OK. I hope you still do.'

Again she paused. This was her boss talking. But he wouldn't be her boss in Bath. He wouldn't be anyone's boss. Neutral ground, she'd said, and neutral ground was what he'd found.

'Do you?' he said.

'In principle, yes.'

'That's terrific. I'll find some really good hotel and—'

She heard Hilly on the stairs and said, 'Fine. Right. I've got to go now. Bye.'

She put the receiver down and Hilly came into the bedroom. 'What did Tom want?'

'He was telling me about a conference next week.'

'Do you have to go?'

'I think so.'

Here it was, the beginning of the lies that would have to be told.

'Can I come with you?'

'No, darling, I can't take you to a conference.'

'Where is it?'

'In Bath.'

'I'd like to go to Bath.'
'I'll take you there one day. We'll all go.'
'Is Tom going?'
'Yes.'
'I like Tom.'
'I'm glad. I like him too.'

9

Taplin had bought an evening paper and was in the sitting room trying to read it. He had read the same story over and over without taking it in. It was almost nine o'clock in the evening and he had been reading the paper since six. In the prison it was almost time for lights out. Here the sun had only just set and the evening was balmy and golden. He wasn't appreciative of the weather or the light; he had not noticed either.

He heard a car in Mulberry Street and, as he had done before, he got to his feet and looked out of the window. He felt his stomach twist. Yes, this time it was hers.

He watched her get out. She must know he was in the house, or at least expect him to be, yet she was as deliberate as she could be. She brought out the two medium-sized suitcases from the back of the car. These, he knew, contained the cosmetics she sold. She placed them on the pavement. Then she brought out a plastic shopping bag and placed it next to the suitcases. She locked the car, making sure of each door. She picked up the suitcases and the shopping bag and brought them to the door of the house. The window at which Taplin was standing was not more than a few feet from her. She looked at him. He raised his hand and smiled. She turned away and opened the door and moved in her luggage.

He came into the passage. 'Betty?'

She did not reply. Instead she carried her luggage along the passage. He followed. 'Betty? Did you mix up the dates?' He had forgotten how small and slim she was. 'Did you?'

'No, I didn't mix up the dates or forget you were coming, if that's what you mean.'

She put the suitcases down in the hall against one wall. 'They'll have to stay here,' she said. 'They're too heavy to carry upstairs.'

He moved forward. 'Here, let me.'

She said, 'I don't want you to touch them.' He checked and she said, 'I don't want you to touch any of my things.'

'All right.'

'It's my turn now.'

'Your turn?'

'In the kitchen. Didn't you read the rules?'

'Betty, listen, I can understand how you might be feeling. Anyone would feel like this—'

'Just read the rules and abide by them.'

'Good Lord, we've been apart for two years. I did something terrible and I—'

She pushed past him into the kitchen. He followed her but she stopped in the doorway. 'I'm going to cook my supper.'

'I bought us a couple of steaks.'

'I don't want your steak!'

She was dressed in a sober dark suit and it showed her legs which had always been good. And there was the small bulge of her breasts and her narrow waist swelling out into her buttocks and thighs.

'Betty, listen to me.'

'No, you listen to me! This is my time in the kitchen. It's in the rules if you'd read them.'

'What rules?'

'I left them on your bed. You must have seen them.'

'I didn't see anything of the sort. Rules? What sort of rules?'

'How we are to live together in this house. Together but apart if you understand me.'

'Betty, this is—'

'Let me finish. You have certain times in the kitchen and the bathroom upstairs. You also have the sitting room and your bedroom down here. I won't come into either of those rooms. You don't come into my bedroom or my sitting room. The only rooms we share are the bathroom and the kitchen and we have separate times for those.'

'I can't believe what I'm hearing! Betty, please listen to me. I realise what you've been through but I've been through something too, you know. Prison isn't just a rest home.'

She didn't seem to hear him. She said, 'I need the bathroom before I go out in the morning and when I come home at night. The times are down in the rules. I also want the kitchen then too. You've got the rest of the day to cook your food and use the bathroom.'

'For God's sake, I don't want to live separately like this! What's the matter with living like we used to live?'

'Everything. Now it's my turn in the kitchen.'

She closed the door. He stood for a moment in the passageway and then turned slowly into the living room and sat down on the sofa. He had known there was resentment and anger – why else give him his own quarters? – but he had not considered that their lives would be totally separate.

He and Betty had, until he lost his job, lived close lives. They had done things together. There had been the training sessions at the gym, the time they had bought bicycles and used them in town on Sundays, the swimming club, the holidays in Brittany. It had been such a good life!

He'd first met her when she'd come to him looking for a small flat when she was working at the store. He'd been impressed by her appearance. He didn't have much for her to look at then, but when something came up, he would go into the store to tell her. In fact, he used to make up excuses to go in and talk to her. In the store she was fantastic in a filmy black uniform, heavily made-up. That's what he remembered most from those early days, the smoothness of her skin and the make-up. Then he saw her without make-up after she had moved into a flat, and he thought she looked even prettier.

Remembering her, remembering them together, brought tears to the back of his eyes. This was no way to live. Not the way she planned it. He went into the kitchen. She was sitting at the table reading the paper and eating what looked like a TV dinner. In her hand she had a six-inch kitchen knife. He paused. The sight of it frightened him. He saw in his mind's eye how she had come at him once, stabbing with a knife very like this one. Fortunately he had managed to twist it out of her hand before he had been cut.

Now, he said: 'Betty, we can't live like this.'

She cut a piece of chicken and chewed it and then said, 'How do you want to live, Ivor?'

'Like we lived before. Oh, I know we can't do that immediately but it'll come. But not if we live separately and don't talk.'

'What do you want to talk about?'

'Us.'

'There is no us.'

'That's not true.'

She stood up sharply and he took some paces back. The knife had frightened him again. 'You can't damage someone and then say, "Sorry let's make up".'

'I've paid for that. And, God, I am sorry.'

'You might have paid what's called your debt to society, but that doesn't help me. Can't you see what you did?' She touched her cheek with her finger. 'Look at that! The bone was smashed there. I still can't feel anything. And look at my eye!'

'I can't see anything the matter with your eye.'

'You must be blind then. It's lower than the other!'

'That's your imagination, Betty. Your eye is still just the same. You've always had lovely eyes.'

'And this!' She tapped the bridge in the centre of her upper teeth.

'Yes, I know. But you can't see any difference. They just look like your own teeth.'

She shook her head as though to dismiss their discussion and then she said, 'Money – that's what we *can* talk about. You owe me more than twelve thousand pounds and I want it.'

'Twelve thousand! How can I possibly owe you that?'

'When I came to the prison to see you—'

'You didn't come often, Betty.'

'I wouldn't have come at all except it was business. But when I came and we talked about the house you said you didn't want to sell it.'

'It was the only thing we had, the only possession I was looking forward to seeing again. All my other things – clothes, stereo, all that stuff – I didn't even think about. I wanted you and the house. It's part of what we've got together.'

'I'll tell you something, Ivor, if the house hadn't been in your name only, I'd have sold it. That's never going to happen to me again.'

'Well, we're not selling it. Listen, we loved this house and we—'

'Love it? Christ, I hate it!'

'You don't really mean that. You always said you loved it.'

'You don't get it, do you? This is yours! I hate anything that's yours!'

He was silent then and she said, 'Money, Ivor. Twelve thousand quid. So you go and sign on the dole and you give me that money.'

'I'll sign on all right but I'll need something. You can have the rest.'

'I want it all. It's going to take long enough to pay me back as it is. Or you can sell the house and pay me.'

At the back of his mind was the thought that if they lost the house it would be the end of them. He had seen this happen all too often in his working years. When a couple had an argument and sold the house that was the end of them. It was as though the last tie – even counting the children – was broken and they simply did not need each other any more. The house was a symbol of the good in their lives.

'I'm not selling the house. We'll manage somehow. There's housing benefit, you know, from Social Services. That'll pay the mortgage, or some of it. I'll get onto them tomorrow.' How was he to tell her that thinking of the house and his return to it was the only thing that had kept him from going insane in prison?

'I don't want to talk to you. It's my time in the kitchen. I don't really want to talk to you at all, Ivor. I thought of doing that, you know, just not talking to you but things would have become difficult. If we shared the house as we are now we'd have had to be writing notes to each other and that would have been boring. But I don't want to talk to you. And I don't want you in the kitchen when it's my turn. Understand?'

He saw the knife move in her hand and he thought he had said enough.

'Yes, I understand, Betty. I'm sure things will come all right.'

As he turned to go he noticed that the plastic shopping

bag on the table had collapsed onto its side and he could see a bottle of gin and one of tonic. He had wondered whether she was still drinking; now he knew.

He sat in the sitting room – his sitting room – looking at the paper again until he knew she had left the kitchen. He went in, cooked his steak and ate it, washed his dishes and cleared away, then he went to his bedroom. He lay back against the pillows fully dressed and read the rules. Times and turns were set out in detail, even to the day the rubbish was collected. He was the one to take it out onto the pavement; she would bring the empty wheelie bin back.

Prison had weakened him in some ways, toughened him in others, but it hadn't helped him to plan his behaviour in a situation like this. He knew he must remain calm and understanding. This would all pass. They needed each other too much to allow it to continue for any length of time. She'd get over her feelings, he was certain of that.

Later, after he had undressed and got into bed, he heard her walking up and down on the floor above him. He was used to the noise of prisoners sleeping or trying to sleep: the coughing and grunting, the swearing and moaning, and sometimes yelling. But he wasn't used to this soft thudding as she walked. It was what she used to do when things were bad. There would be this move-ment, the thud . . . thud . . . backwards and forwards. Usually after she had been drinking. It gave a sense of foreboding. Of something portentous about to happen. He got out of bed and went to the door. There was no key. There wasn't even a lock.

Who ever heard of locking a dining-room door?

92

★ ★ ★

Henry Vernon BA, LLB (Cantab), formerly Mr Justice Vernon sometime circuit court judge in Lesotho, southern Africa, was no expert in photocopying machines or computers. It would not be exaggerating to say that he was not an expert in any known piece of technological office equipment, with the exception of the pencil sharpener. Bannister, Burleigh & Bleache had several pieces of modern office equipment in their nineteenth-century offices, and they also had a pencil sharpener. In the short time Henry had worked for them he had never seen the pencil sharpener in action and longed to use it. But he had never seen any pencils either. Instead he seemed to spend his time with the photocopier. This, by comparison with the latest developments in photocopying of which Henry was not aware, was also nineteenth century. It needed standing over and could only make a few copies at a time. It also needed someone to put in and take out the sheet being copied. It could not load itself automatically.

The photocopying was endless. It had started on the first day, when Miss Moberly had dumped a pile of documents on his desk and said with a thin smile, 'For Mr Baker. Two copies of each. And he says ASAP.'

Henry had not heard the acronym before and he took some time to work it out. He had a lot of time for thought because he had to stand over the machine.

Just when he thought he had completed photocopying every document in the building, Miss Moberly – he had established that it was Miss – would arrive with another pile.

Henry was sick of photocopying and sick of Miss Moberly and generally sick of the job he had taken. He had never considered for a moment that joining a legal firm would have so little to do with the law. He had assumed that the office work in which he was engulfed would quickly come to an end as the courts returned from vacation. This had so far not happened. The day before, there had been a slight flurry as a case came up on the Warned List – the list from which substitute cases could suddenly be brought forward – and the barrister originally briefed was unavailable. It was possible that Henry would have to read the brief and help a barrister who had read it perhaps only on the train that morning. But nothing came of it. The case was postponed before it reached court and Henry was confined once more to his office in the passageway which was dominated by the photocopying machine.

'This is what some office boy should be doing,' he told himself, as he inserted the endless sheets of paper.

But he also told himself that sitting at home or playing a hundred-up in the club was even more frustrating. He consoled himself with the thought that other Warned List cases would come up and would not be postponed, and then he would find himself in the place he liked and understood best – a courtroom.

Miss Moberly came down the passageway. 'Oh, Mr Vernon, we're missing the original of that.'

She handed him one of the copies of a conveyancing document he had made.

'I put the originals together,' he said. 'I gave you everything.'

94

'Well, it's not there. Perhaps you'd be good enough to look for it.'

It was the prissy way she said it that annoyed Henry, as though he were a recalcitrant schoolboy.

'Have you looked in your own office?' he said.

'Yes, I have. And Mr Baker's.'

She stood waiting while Henry looked on his desk and under it and beside it and on the filing cabinet and on the floor behind it.

Miss Moberly watched him for some moments and then said, 'Have you looked on the machine?'

'What machine?' It was said with immense irritation.

'The copying machine.'

'There's nothing—' He raised the lid. 'Oh . . . here it is. Sorry about that. It must have been the last one.'

She took it and turned away without thanks and left him feeling the weight of her contempt.

10

'There's a funny man,' Hilly said.

Anne was getting breakfast. It was Saturday morning and neither Watch nor her father were upstairs yet. Since this was not a school or work morning, things were taken slowly and in a relaxed manner. What made it even more relaxed was that, like Sunday, it was a no-tea, no-cooked-breakfast morning. This was at Anne's request, for she liked cooking for Hilly and herself at weekends and now she was making breakfast pancakes to be sprinkled with brown sugar and lemon juice. They were at present Hilly's breakfast favourites.

'Mummy. There's a funny man.'

'Where?'

'Out in the street.'

'Funny like a clown?'

'No, not like a clown! He just looks funny.'

'You mean strange.'

'And he's looking at our house.'

'Come and have your pancakes while they're hot.'

Hilly came in from the sitting room and attacked the pancakes. Anne had made enough for Henry and Watch if they wanted them and now she began to pick at them. She finished one, then two, then licked her fingers and took her coffee into the sitting room. The venetian blinds had been half-opened and the morning sun was streaming through them. Hilly, with her plate in her hands, followed her into the room.

'See him?'

'Where?'

'On the bench under the tree.'

'Oh yes.'

'See, he's looking at our house.'

'No, darling, he's just sitting there in the morning sun. Lots of people— Hang on, I think I know him. It's . . . yes, it's a person called Taplin, Ivor Taplin.'

'From the prison?'

'Yes, from the prison. He went out yesterday. I think, or the day before.' She frowned. What was he doing outside the house?

'Is he a bad fairy?' They had been reading that story the night before.

'No. More like a sad fairy.'

'Does he know we live here?'

'Of course not.' Then she thought: Why not? All he had to do was look us up in the phone book.

'What does he want?'

'I shouldn't think he wants anything. He's just sitting on a public bench. Everyone's got a right to do that.'

'But why outside our house?'

'He lives in Kingstown. Probably having a good look round so he'll get to know the place again. He had a job once, selling houses.' She heard her voice say these things but didn't believe what she was saying.

'Some more pancakes?' she asked her daughter.

Hilly shook her head. 'Did you know him?'

'Not very well. I saw him a few times. He had an upset tummy like Watch gets sometimes.'

They wandered back into the kitchen. 'Apple juice?' Anne said. 'Or tropical?'

'Tropical. Does it really have mangoes in it?'

'That's what it says on the label.'

Hilly went to the kitchen window that overlooked the back of the house. 'Grandpa's digging in the garden. Shall I take him a tropical?'

'He likes apple juice. Take him a glass if you like.'

Hilly went downstairs clutching a glass and Anne began tidying the kitchen. She put the dishes in the washer. Then she moved back into the living room and looked once more through the venetian blind. Taplin was still there. He had hardly changed his position. And Hilly was right; he seemed to be looking at the house.

But was he really? Couldn't he just be sitting there taking the morning sun as she had explained to Hilly? Should she go out and talk to him? Or should she just forget about the whole thing?

But she couldn't forget it. Memories of her induction weeks came back to her, with the warnings of what to do and what *not* to do in the prison service. In other words, how to behave around prisoners. And of them all, the one she remembered most clearly was: was do not form any sort of relationship with a prisoner on release.

But going out and saying 'Good morning' could hardly be construed as a relationship.

She saw Taplin get up from the bench and thought with relief that he was leaving and that nothing need be done or said. But all he did was move along the bench to a patch of shade.

For a moment she considered the possibility of phoning Tom. But what could he say? He would only tell her to ignore him or phone the police. Or he might even come himself and warn Taplin off, which would be embarrassing, for all the man had done was sit down on a bench.

Should she just keep an eye on him without doing anything? But that would mean hiding here at the corner of the Venetian blinds like some peeper in the movies.

She thought of Taplin coming to her for his examination and what had followed: the pathetic gratitude he had felt towards her when he should have felt quite the opposite. He was a sad fairy; no doubt about that. And the chess board in her mind having made the substitution of 'sad' for 'bad' seemed to help her make up her mind. A 'sad' person posed no threat, so she opened the front door and went out into the street.

He saw her immediately and rose.

'Good morning, Mr Taplin.' She saw his eyes widen with surprise and pleasure. He clearly hadn't been called 'mister' for a long time.

'I was just looking at the street,' he said hurriedly, as though he needed an excuse for sitting where he was.

'Yes, I thought you were.'

'I've sold houses here. Just wanted to see how it was, you know . . . if it was still as good as it had been.'

'And is it?'

'Oh yes. You'd never have to wait long for a buyer here. Expensive houses.'

'Yes. Too expensive for me, but—'

'I didn't mean it that way.' He looked suddenly crest-fallen.

'Of course you didn't. Sorry, that was my fault. No, what I meant was that my father and I shared the costs. He has a flat in the house.'

He seemed too embarrassed to reply and she smiled and said, 'But if we ever sell, we'll get in touch with you.'

'I'd hardly know what to do now if someone came to me with a property for sale. Anyway, I hope you never do.'

'Oh?'

'It might mean that you were moving from the city and leaving the prison – and that would be bad for the prison. I thought you were the only human being there.'

'That's not quite true but it's a nice thing to hear.' The well of guilt she had felt about him in the prison now seemed to fill again and she heard her voice saying, 'Would you like a coffee, Mr Taplin? I've just made some.'

A look of wonderment replaced the confusion in his eyes. 'I'd love one.'

He really had an educated voice, she thought, and had answered the question just as a friend or acquaintance might. But even so she was amazed at what she had done. There was no going back, though.

He followed her across the street and into the house. He stopped at the sitting-room door and looked in.

'Lovely room,' he said.

'It goes through to the kitchen,' she said. 'My father lives downstairs but we thought we'd share the kitchen so we built a big one where the dining room had been. Now the two rooms join.'

'Open plan,' Taplin said. 'Just the thing these days.'

They went into the kitchen and talked about the house a little more. He sat at the table and Anne stood by the windows. He was interested and knowledgeable and she said, 'You don't really mean what you implied, about not knowing what to do in the housing business?'

'Not completely. Anyway, no one's likely to give me a property to sell.'

'You never know.'

Then he said, 'But something had better happen and it had better be soon.'

'Oh?'

'My wife Betty says I owe her a lot of money.'

Anne decided she didn't want to get into that and said, 'Are you settling down all right?'

'If you can be married and a bachelor at the same time then I suppose you could say I was settling down.'

She didn't ask him to expand on that either, but he did anyway. It suddenly poured out of him in waves. He told her about getting home and finding the house changed, and about walking the streets and coming down to this street and seeing her family. And he told her about buying the steaks and going home and waiting for Betty, and then hearing about the parameters that would frame their new life and the money he owed her.

'I don't want to live like that.' She heard a note of desperation in his voice.

'I'm sure everything will work out.' She winced at the bromide.

'I hope so. She says I owe her twelve thousand quid and I haven't a hope in hell of paying her.'

'Twelve thousand? Goodness, that's a lot.' This time her tone had a kind of winsomeness that she loathed.

She wanted this intimate conversation to stop there but he said, 'She paid the mortgage when I was in the nick. She didn't say so but I imagine she had to work twice as hard. Now she says I must give her my welfare cheque. That'll leave me with nothing!' it was said angrily and without self-pity.

Anne said, 'Wouldn't the best solution be to sell your house?'

'I'll never sell that house. Not if I can help it. Or anyway not for some years. In the eighties, house prices went through the roof and then they dropped back. I'm . . . we're . . . not quite in negative equity but damn close. I suppose it would depend on who valued the house. But things'll take off soon in the housing market. They always do. It's ups and downs . . . Hello.'

Hilly came up the stairs. He was smiling at her. She said hello and then took Anne's hand.

'This is Hilary,' Anne said. 'This is Mr Taplin.'

'I saw you the other day,' Taplin said. 'A dark gentleman brought you home in a car.'

'Mr Taplin was looking at the houses in the street,' Anne said. 'He's an expert in houses.'

'You have a lovely house,' Taplin said. 'You're very lucky to live here.'

Hilly, usually with a comment on most things, was

silent and Anne, worried that the conversation might languish, returned to what they had been talking about. 'I'm sure the market will pick up,' she said, 'and that will mean there'll be jobs for estate agents.'

'But what happens until then?' Taplin said. 'I've thought of doing some painting and decorating. I became very good at that during my lay-off from work.'

Anne said to Hilly, 'Mr Taplin is going to be looking for a job like a lot of other people.'

Taplin said, more to himself than to Anne, 'And how do you get a job when you've got a prison record? No one's ever answered that.'

'He could do the windows,' Hilly said.

'What?' Anne said.

Hilly pointed. 'The sitting-room windows. You're always saying they need doing.'

'I noticed them from the street,' Taplin said. 'Some of the wood looks rotten where the paint's been flaking. If you don't do something about them soon you'll have a big bill.'

'Oh, I'll have them looked at one day.'

Taplin said, 'Look, you were good to me in the nick. Let me do them for you.'

'No, I—'

'I won't charge you. I owe you a great debt for listening to me and helping me. It would give me pleasure.'

'Absolutely not. I don't think I—'

'And they really need doing.'

The conversation came to a sudden stop. Anne was experiencing more than the usual guilt; now she was feeling as though she was directly letting him down.

She said, 'I could never let you do them for nothing. That just wouldn't—'

'All right, look, I'll do them for six pounds an hour. All you would be paying for is my time. And that's about a third of what anyone else would charge. I'll remove all the old paint and cut out any rotten wood and replace it and then I'll give them a good primer and a couple of undercoats and a couple of top coats and they'll last for years.'

'Well, I don't know.' Anne suddenly felt that things were moving away from her but didn't know how to stop them.

'Can we have them painted orange?' Hilly said.

Taplin smiled. 'With pink spots?'

Anne said, 'Just black, I think.'

Taplin nodded. 'Black would be best.' There was a silence. A deal had been struck. He looked at Hilly and smiled again and then said to Anne, 'If we'd had a kid, none of this would have happened. You don't know how lucky you are.'

Anne ran her fingers through Hilly's hair. 'Oh yes, I do.'

They watched him go off down the street. He had promised to come on Monday and Anne had said, 'Oh, there's no hurry. Any time.' When she thought about that now, she knew she was trying to postpone things indefinitely. She seemed to have got herself into a situation she didn't want to be in, but told herself finally not to be silly.

Her father, on the other hand, implied that she *had*

been silly. More than implied it. 'Of course I know the windows need doing, the whole place needs doing. We agreed on that when we bought it. We also agreed we didn't have the money but postponed it on a when and if basis.'

'Good lord, I'm not having the whole house done, just the outside of the sitting-room windows. And anyway, I'm paying for it and he's not charging much.'

'It's not the cost, it's the man himself,' Henry said. 'I don't like ex-prisoners working around the house.'

'I'm not thrilled either but it seemed the least I could do. He's had a bad time. I've told you his background.'

'You sound as if you're entering a plea of mitigation.'

'I'm not entering a plea at all – and stop being the judge all the time! We the public are always being asked to help released prisoners. Give them jobs. Be fair to them. Treat them like everyone else. Or else they just revert to what they were doing before.'

'Which was beating up women.'

'*A* woman – his wife. After she had committed numerous assaults on him.'

'How do you know? Was it ever led in evidence in court?'

'No.'

'Well, then, he's being his own witness.'

'That may be so but I believed him. For goodness sake, you have to believe people some of the time! The world couldn't function otherwise. I treated him in prison and I heard what he had to say and I believed him. All he's going to do is fix some windows outside. It's no big deal!'

'I hope you're right.'
'Anyway, Watch is here all day.'
'Yes, that's true. I'd forgotten that.'
'Well, I hadn't.'
And that's how it was left.

11

'Yes, Les, what is it?'

Les Foley put his head and shoulders round Anne's door and said, 'Payne wants to see you, Doc.'

'Tell him to put in his request in the usual way.'

'He says you won't see him if he does.'

Anne was working on a report for a Crown Court case that was riddled with complexities and did not want to be interrupted.

'I've a good mind not to see him in any circumstances. Do you know what he wants? Is he ill or does he just want to talk?'

'Says it's about security.'

'Oh.'

'Could by an SIR.'

'Payne?'

'Might have overheard something.'

'Oh God! All right. I'll see him, but not for half an hour.'

When Les did bring him over she had still not finished the report and her head was full of it.

'Cheers, Doc,' Payne said, his acne-scarred face breaking into a smile.

'This isn't a social visit, Payne. I'm not sure I want to see you after last time, but you told Officer Foley it was important so what's this vital piece of information?'

Payne made a little business of looking over his shoulder and, irritated, Anne said, 'No one's listening.'

'Prison walls have ears, Doc. You heard that saying?'

'No, I haven't. Please go on.'

'Well, it's about Taplin.'

'I thought you told Mr Foley it was about security.'

'Well, this is security. It's the security of someone outside.'

'All right, go on.'

'Well, we used to talk, see. Lots of time in the nick for that. And he needed someone to talk to 'cos his wife hardly ever came to see him. Know what I mean?'

'Yes. Go on.'

'Well, we had talks about everything you can think of. Houses . . . used to talk a bit about houses. Buying them and selling and things like that. That was his job. Estate agent.'

'Yes, I know.'

'And he liked talking about his own house. Loved that bleedin' house. To me a house is a house. Know what I mean? Place to eat and kip—'

'Please get to the point, Payne. I'm very busy today.'

'Yeah. Right. Well, when he wasn't talking about his house he was talking about his wife, see. And he tells me about her and he tells me about how he wanted kids. Mad about kids, he was. But his wife won't give him none.' He leaned back and stared at her.

'So?'

'So why d'you think he duffs her up?'

'Because she didn't have a baby?'

'Got to be! That's what happened. He wants kids, she doesn't. Biff! Bang! Wallop!'

'Oh, come on, Payne.'

'It's the truth! I'm telling you the honest truth!'

'Like you told me your mother was still alive when she died some years ago?'

'You must've misunderstood me, Doc. I would never say nothing like that.'

'All right, I misunderstood you. Is that all you've got to tell me?'

'That's only the background, Doc.'

'Well, I don't really want to hear any more. This is all just supposition and—'

'Hang on, hang on, I ain't told you the best part yet. Taplin says to me . . . he says he's going to kill her.'

'Who's he going to kill?'

'His wife, Betty.'

'Why?'

''Cos she ain't giving him any kids.'

'He told you this?'

'Cross my heart.'

'When?'

'A few days ago. He says, "Ronnie, me old mate" – that's what he called me, his old mate – he says, "I'm going to do her in. If I got to serve time for her, so be it. But I ain't going to live with her no more." That's what he said. Exact words.'

'Because she wouldn't have a baby?'

'Yep. That's it.'

'Tell me something, Payne. Why have you come to *me* with this story? Why not go to the Governor?'

'Well . . .'

'Is it because you think I could put in a word that might mean a reduction in your sentence?'

'Well, you done that for Taplin.'

'I'm stopping this right now.'

'Hang on a minute, Doc. I mean – be reasonable.'

'I will be reasonable. I won't report you to the Governor. But equally I won't do anything about this lot of rubbish you've told me. Now I'm going to ask Mr Foley to take you back.' She rang her desk buzzer and Les Foley came into the room. 'Payne's going back now.'

'Hang on a minute, Doc. I ain't fin—'

'Let's be having you, Payne,' Les Foley said, and with great reluctance Ronnie Payne was taken back to his cell.

Anne tried to go back to her report but her mind was full of blood and mayhem. There was a knock on the door and Tom came in, 'Finished?'

'You mean with Payne or with this bloody report?' She tapped the paper. 'I don't think he's psychotic at all. He's a fantasist all right but I think he's having us on. A bit like Payne.'

'What did he want anyway?'

'He's got some load of nonsense about murder threats. It's all to do with an obsession he has that somehow I managed to get his cell mate's sentence reduced.'

Tom wasn't really interested but nodded his head and waited until she had finished and then he said, 'I've found a place.'

'What?'

'Hotel in Bath.'

'Oh!'

There was a subtext to the exclamation that he immediately registered. They had never brought their private lives into the prison. He raised his hand and said, 'I'll ring you tonight and tell you about it. Sounds good though.' Then he was gone.

When Anne drove home that evening the sun was shining brightly, the air was hot and Kingstown was displaying itself as a beautiful old cathedral city with a dusty summer patina. She passed the Cathedral and saw the tourist buses parked at the bottom of the High Street. This was the only problem about living in history, too many people wanted to come along and poke about in it. She came to the top of Castle Street and turned into it and thought for the umpteenth time how beautiful it was and how lucky she was to live there. Then she tried to remember who had said that recently? Oh yes, it had been Taplin talking to Hilly.

And there he was!

She saw the ladder first. It was propped against the front wall of her house and Taplin was halfway up it. He was working at the black paint on the frame of one of the sitting-room windows, chipping and scraping and rubbing with a wire brush.

She got out of her car and greeted him. He came down to the pavement. His face was spotted by small flecks of black paint and so were his hands and forearms. He was dressed in jeans and a white shirt, and over them wore a cream carpenter's apron with a large pocket in front for his tools.

He said, 'I should really use a blow torch to burn away the old paint but I don't trust them. I've known houses burn down because sparks have got into old wood and then been fanned hours later by the wind.'

She had not forgotten he was coming but at the same time had rather hoped he wouldn't. Now that he was there she had to make the best of the arrangement.

'I'm going to cut out the rotten wood and replace it. Then I'll put the primer on.' He paused for a moment. 'Have you got an account at any of the hardware shops?' She could hear the embarrassment in his tone and knew what was coming next.

'No. You'll need money, won't you?'

'I'm afraid so. But I'll bring you back receipts.'

'Oh, I wasn't—'

'No, no, I'm sure you weren't but I've got to be professional. I mean, this is the only sort of work I might be able to get. If I do yours well, you may tell your friends. Word of mouth. Best advertising of all.'

'How much would you need?'

'Twenty pounds should do it. That'll be the paint as well. Of course, that's only these outside windows. If you wanted me to do the insides of the windows and the other rooms as well I'll need more.'

'Yes, well . . . we can talk about that later.' She gave him twenty pounds.

'I'll bring you the receipts tomorrow,' he said.

She went into the house. The family was in the big kitchen. Watch was cooking, her father was reading *The*

Times and Hilly was watching TV.

Anne kissed Hilly and tapped her father on the head and smiled at Watch.

Hilly whispered, 'We're having smoked haddock and eggs. Yuk.'

Henry brought his head out of the newspaper and said, 'I thought we'd have smoked haddock and poached eggs for a change. Watch does them even better than I do.'

'How lovely,' Anne said.

Hilly said, 'We had them last Thursday and I—'

'Friday,' Watch said. 'It was eh-Friday.'

'Well, we haven't had them since last week,' Henry said. 'And I know you all love them. I certainly do. They kept me fit and healthy in the bundu where you can get all sorts of horrors. I remember once, Annie, you went down with that twenty-four-hour vomiting sickness after eat—'

'Please, not when we're about to have supper! Isn't anyone going to give me a glass of wine?'

'You're drinking too much,' Hilly said.

'Listen to the child,' Henry said. 'The problem with Hilly is you don't beat her enough. I used to beat you until you were blue and look how well you've developed.'

Anne poured herself a glass of wine and turned to Watch. 'Did he?'

Watch smiled a small, secretive smile. 'Judge don't let anybody touch you,' he said. 'You had a nanny. A woman from Maseru. She smacked you once and the Judge he said to the woman, "You do that again and I smack you too – but with eh-cricket bat".'

'And did she?'

'Never.'

Henry said, 'Watch just makes up these stories.'

'Mummy! Listen! It's the van.' They could hear the recorded blare of an ice-cream van. 'Can I have one?'

'Not before your supper.'

'Oh, Mummy!'

'I'll make you some. I've got a new recipe. How about that?'

'When?'

'Soon.'

A few moments later there was a knock at the front door.

Anne went, with Hilly just behind her. Taplin was standing on the front step. In his hand he had an ice-cream cone. 'For Miss Hilly,' he said, holding it out to her.

Hilly looked at her mother for permission and Anne nodded and smiled and said, 'That's very nice of you, Ivor. Isn't it, Hilly?'

Hilly nodded. 'Thank you,' she said.

Taplin said, 'I'm off now. See you tomorrow.'

Anne closed the door. Hilly said, 'He called me Miss Hilly.' She tasted the phrase and Anne could see that she liked it.

Later, after Hilly had gone to bed and Watch had gone downstairs to have a bath, Henry said to Anne, 'I still don't like it.'

'Don't like what?'

'This man Taplin, of course. His being here.'

'We've had all that out. You know my feelings.'

'Bloody political correctness, that's what this is all about.'

'Not in the slightest.'

'Well, socially correct then. You've been got at. Just because it's the socially correct thing to help released prisoners, you think you have to be socially correct.'

'No, I don't. Look, Taplin was in for something I hate – abuse within the family. But he was mostly the one abused.'

'And you believe all this rubbish about wives beating up husbands?'

'I'm surprised at you, a judge, making a statement like that.'

'In all my years on the bench I never came across a case of a wife battering a husband. Quite the reverse.'

'OK, that was Africa where women are fifth-class citizens compared to men. But it happens here and it's happening more often.'

He waved a dismissive hand. 'And look at this ice-cream business and calling her Miss Hilly. The bugger's trying to insinuate himself into the family. I say watch the silver and the Canalettos.'

'I gave him twenty pounds for paint – what do you bet he comes tomorrow not only with the paint but with the receipts? Come on, what about a fiver?'

'You can't afford to lose a fiver. Let's make it fifty pence.'

'Done.'

The following day Taplin gave her the receipts and she collected fifty pence from her father.

'What do you say now?' she said.

'I still say watch the silver.'

'We haven't got any.'

'Yes, but does he know that?'

'I'd get back to that book of medieval legal history if I were you. It sounds just the kind of background from which you come.'

But later she said to Taplin, 'It was very kind of you to buy Hilly an ice cream yesterday but I'd rather you didn't. You see, she has a bit of an allergy to dairy products.'

'Oh Lord, I'm sorry,' Taplin said. 'It was just so hot and the van was here.'

'Of course. And it was very nice of you.'

'Don't worry. I won't again.'

She went back into the house worried now at something else: her ability to lie so easily to a man who was just showing a little kindness.

12

It had been a busy morning for Anne, organising her departure, but now she was at last on the road to Bath. First of all there had been Hilly, then there had been Watch, then her father. It had started before morning tea had arrived. She had woken early with a knot of excitement and unease in her stomach. To give herself something to do, she had gone through the carry bag she had packed the night before. She unpacked it and looked at her clothes. All in all, she had thought, no one could have more dreary underwear and nighties and dress-up clothes and dress-down clothes and shoes and handbags than she had. It was a grotty collection and yet when she had bought each item she had thought how nice it was. She began going through her drawers again to see if there wasn't, by some miraculous chance, a sexy black nightie she had forgotten all about.

'What are you doing?' Hilly's muffled voice had come through from her neighbouring bedroom.

'Packing.'

'You woke me up.'

'Sorry, it's nearly morning tea anyway.'

119

Anne closed her drawers. There was no miracle nightie.

'What's the conference about?'

'Prisoners and prisons.'

'Why can't I come?'

'Because it's a school day, the last day of this term, and you wouldn't want to miss that.

'It's a play day. Miss Garth said we don't have to do lessons on the last day.'

'Anyway, you wouldn't be allowed in, and even if you were, you'd be bored stiff.'

Should she buy something exotic? And would Tom notice if she did? It didn't matter if he didn't – well, yes it did, of course it did – but even if he didn't she'd know she was looking good. She decided to buy something in Bath.

A few moments after Hilly had woken, Anne heard Watch on the stairs. 'Tea,' he said as he entered her room. 'Blekfas' half an hour.'

She took the cup and smelled the whiff of iron filings. 'Now is there anything you need to know?' she said.

'Know about eh-what?'

He knew exactly what she meant, she thought. 'Well, you know, about everything. Specially Hilly.'

'I take her to school like I do every day. I fetch her from school like every day. I give her blekfas' and supper. I say good night. I lock the door and I lock the windows and I switch out all the lights . . .'

She laughed. 'I'm sorry, Watch, but you know what a fusser my father is, and I may have inherited the genes. Anyway, you only have to take Hilly today because—'

'Because it is last day of term.'

'Right. And the holidays start.'

He turned away to take Hilly's steely brew into her room but Anne stopped him. 'Watch, is my father all right?'

'How you mean?'

'Well, he seemed all right yesterday, I heard him arguing with Hilly, but he's not been his usual self.'

'I told him he should not work.'

'But he likes it. He hates sitting around here doing nothing.'

'He is too old for that work.'

'If that's the case, you're too old for this work.'

Watch's thin face puckered and his lips pressed together. 'I am younger than the Judge.'

Anne knew he was about three months younger but decided not to press the point. 'I'd forgotten that.' He turned to go again and she said, 'Oh, and Watch, just keep an eye out for Mr Taplin.'

'But he finished. You have eh-paid him.'

'Yes, I know. But just in case.'

She showered and went down to breakfast. Her father was eating a large cooked meal and reading the paper. He put it down and said, 'Well, you're off today. What's this conference all about anyway?'

She knew she was not going to be able to fudge it as she had with Hilly. 'It's on drugs in prisons. There's been a study on whether the focus should be on prophylaxsis or the treatment. We've tried both together and they haven't worked well.'

'So what are you contributing?'

121

She had anticipated this and said, 'Nothing. I'm listening.'

She checked the list of THINGS TO DO which she had stuck on the fridge door and said, 'The hotel number is down here.'

'You've told me that five times already.'

Now, as she drove past Andover on the way to Bath these vignettes came crowding back into her consciousness. Was she really getting as fussy as her father? If that were so she had better take care, for Watch fussed in his own way which would make three fussy adults in one house – and that would be hard for everyone, especially Hilly, to live with.

But in the meantime would Watch and her father be able to cope? Of course they would! They had coped with her when she was a child; they had brought her up. She would be hard put to think of any two men who would be able to cope better with a small girl than those two father figures.

Father figures . . . that was another problem. What Hilly needed was a proper father. Father figures were one thing, real fathers were quite another. Tom had mentioned this more than once, but even he would only be a stepfather. However, with Paul dead that was the best Hilly would ever have, a loving stepfather. And Tom would be that, she was sure.

She remembered the first time she had been to his house out in the woods some miles from Kingstown. It was a strange place to find hidden away in the West Sussex Downs. There was no formal garden, just rough lawn with half a dozen apple trees heavy with fruit.

The house was a beautiful wooden chalet, clearly built a long time ago, and Anne thought it would have looked more natural in Austria or Bavaria. She had stopped on the weed-covered drive and gone up the steps to the wide verandah. The front door was open and she had heard Tom's voice shouting from within.

She had been about to knock on the door but paused. She heard his voice again, this time lower. Finally she had decided to identify herself and he had called, 'I'm up here.'

She had gone in and found a bathroom at the top of the stairs. It was a large square room. A long old-fashioned cast-iron bath stood against one wall. Tom, a towel around his waist, was on his knees beside the bath. In the bath itself, in six inches of water, was a small black-and-tan dachshund. She was looking up with huge appealing eyes.

Tom said to the dog, 'Come on, darling! Up! Up! Get up!'

It was then Anne had seen that the back legs were paralysed.

Tom said, 'You go down to the other end of the bath.' He handed her several pieces of Ryvita. 'Give her a piece when she gets to your end.'

He took the dog to the other end of the bath and raised her onto her back legs. 'Come on. Up! She can if she wants to, she just finds it easier to drag her legs behind her. Show her the biscuit.'

He put his hands in the water and moved the dog's back legs, forcing her to walk down the bath. When she arrived Anne gave her a small piece of biscuit. Tom

picked her up and put her back at the other end, and
said to the dog, 'Come on now, try it on your own, you
lazy hound.'

But the back legs buckled under her and she began to
pull herself along the bath by her forelegs.

'What's her name?' Anne said.

'Beanie. She used to sleep in a baked bean box.' He
worked her legs again as Beanie moved down the bath to
get at the biscuit Anne was holding. 'She's a greedy little
thing, that's why I have to give her slimming biscuits.
Otherwise she'd put on weight.'

'What happened to her?'

'She had an accident. Broke a vertebra. But she's got
feeling in her legs and tail.'

'How long has she been like this?'

'Three months. We'll get her right. OK, that's enough.'
He scooped Beanie out of the bath, wrapped the shivering body in a towel and said to Anne, 'Come downstairs
and we'll find a drink.'

On the ground floor he waved her to a large armchair.
Still clutching the dog he went off to get a bottle and
glasses.

She looked round. The kitchen, with a dining table
and chairs, was on the left side of the front door, and on
the right, the living room where she was sitting. There
were no lights on and the place had a chilly look and a
chilly feel.

The furniture looked like a job lot bought at a car-
boot sale – functional but lacking in warmth. It had
reminded her of the way her father had furnished his
retirement cottage and when she had mentioned her

thoughts to him he had said, 'Men without women always live like this.'

Tom came back with a bottle of white wine and glasses. Then he spread a towel on his lap and sat Beanie on top of it. He began to work gently on her back legs, pressing her feet so that she would have to use her muscles and resist his pressure. He said, 'Her muscle tone's quite good but she's just not making the connection that by using her legs she could walk.'

It was Hilly who helped to make that connection which started Beanie on the road to recovery. The next time Anne had gone out to Tom's house Hilly had come with her. Hilly, of course, had fallen for Beanie the instant she'd seen her. First she had patted her then she had asked if she could take her outside. A little later, Anne and Tom had watched from the window and seen a strange sight. Hilly and Beanie were on the wet damp grass. Hilly had a piece of muffin in her fingers and was offering it to the dog. Beanie had risen on all four legs and was stretching for the food. As they watched, Hilly moved the piece of muffin slightly further away from her. Beanie tried to reach it, took one pace, and then collapsed.

'Oh God,' Anne said. 'Poor little thing.'

'No, no!' She felt Tom's hand on her arm gripping tightly. 'Watch.'

Slowly Beanie pulled herself up again into a standing position and Hilly gave her the piece of muffin.

'She's never done that before.' Tom had run out of the house and down the steps. Anne followed.

He had squatted down beside the two of them and

questioned Hilly. Had Beanie done it by herself? How many times? Had Hilly lifted her up?'

Hilly had looked at him in surprise. 'She doesn't like the wet grass on her tummy.'

It was as though he had been struck on the head. 'My God, of course! Dachshunds hate the cold, especially on their tummies. Go on, try again.'

It had worked again and Tom had called Hilly a genius. It was a moment Anne would always remember.

So that had been a brilliant start. Tom had liked Hilly, Hilly had liked Tom – and there was Beanie.

But was that everything? It was one thing to make sure that Hilly liked Tom and vice versa but it was she, Anne, who was going to have to live with him, and much more closely than Hilly. Did she want to? Did she want to live with anyone that close?

The answer was yes. But was it Tom?

She remembered going to his house once and seeing Stephanie there and wondering if he was having an affair – if that was the word – with his ex-wife. She remembered how jealous she had felt. Then, only recently, she had thought he might have been offered another job and might leave Kingstown, and that had caused a stab of anxiety.

So the answer to that other question must be a yes, too.

They'd never been to bed. They'd come close but it had never happened. She hadn't been to bed with anyone since the muscular Clive had departed her life.

By the time she had passed Andover she was thinking more about Tom than about her home, and by the time she reached Bath she could have been in another world from the one in which lived her father and Hilly and Watch.

Ivor Taplin woke that morning trying to remember who he was and where he was. He had become used to waking with the echo of the screw's voice in his head: the 'good mornings', the rattle of the keys and the chains, the slamming open of the doors, all accompanied by the grating noise of Ronnie Payne's breathing.

Then the understanding came: he was in the dining room of his own house and it was now his bedroom. The light coming in the window had a greyish quality and he knew it must still be very early. He looked at his watch; it wasn't six o'clock yet. If he went into the kitchen now he would be well ahead of the schedule. Betty's time was eight to nine, his any other time. The long Friday stretched ahead of him. What was he going to do? How was he going to use up time until he and Betty resumed, partially to start with, their married life? For he had no doubt that this would happen. He mustn't push it. That's what he'd done last night – not pushed much, just enough to make her irritated with him. But, Christ, no one could blame him.

Doc Vernon had paid him for his work and he had wanted to give Betty something, a present on his return from prison. He had gone to a jewellers and bought her a pair of earrings. OK, they weren't diamonds or amethysts but turquoise glass. But they were pretty. He had gone into the kitchen when she was having her supper and pushed the little box onto the table and said, 'These are for you.'

She'd been reading the evening paper and had not looked up.

'A present,' he said. 'I got paid today.'

She said, 'This is my time.'

'Yes, I know. But I wanted to give them to you.'

'The times are written down. I told you to read them.'

'I did, but I didn't think you'd mind this once.'

She was eating what looked like grilled fish and now she took her fork and pushed the little jeweller's box until it fell off the table. Taplin bent and picked it up.

'I'll keep it for you,' he said.

She said, 'Have you signed on yet with the Social Security?'

'Yes,' he lied.

'You'll get your first cheque in two weeks. I want the money then.'

She emphasised her point with the kitchen knife he had seen the first day he'd been back.

'And have you registered with the parole office?'

'Yes,' he lied again.

'Just before you were released a Mr Hawksley, a parole officer, came to see me, to talk to me about you. He said you were out on licence and if you did anything to me or tried to do anything – what he meant was even if you thought about doing anything to me – you'd go back to prison.'

'But why should I do anything to you?'

'You did before. Or have you forgotten?'

'God no, I'll never forget. All I can say is you wore me down.'

'Wore you down?' She had grown her hair so that it

128

partially covered the small scar on her cheekbone and now she brushed it back. 'Wore you down how?'

'You know what I mean.'

'You're not going to start that again, are you?'

'What?'

'Lying about me.'

'I'm not lying, I never lied.'

'You know something, Ivor? I told Mr Hawksley that part of it – how you lied when you said I attacked you. You know what he said?'

'No.'

'He said all the wife-beaters say that.'

He had taken the earrings and gone to his sitting room and switched on the TV but he hadn't been able to concentrate and switched it off. He heard her do her washing up and then go upstairs. He heard her TV come on. Then he heard her go to the bathroom; heard the tap run. That meant she didn't have any tonic, that she was probably just drinking gin and water as she did sometimes. After a while he'd gone to bed himself and while he was trying to read he had thought of the knife and gone into the kitchen and opened the drawer. And there it was. A long thin blade which they both used for peeling vegetables and cutting meat. He remembered that she had bought it years before and that it had cost quite a lot for a knife – but in those days they'd had quite a lot. He took the knife and put it in the crockery cupboard. Not perfect but it would have to do.

Now, lying in his bed on this Friday morning, he thought of the long day ahead. All right, he would sign on at both places. That would kill some of the time. If

the day was good he would go down and sit by the river.
If he saw someone fishing he'd ask him about it. Maybe
he could get interested. On the other hand he might go
down to Doc Vernon's house to check on the work and
ask her if she knew anyone else who might want work
done. Perhaps she would give him another job; perhaps
he would see the kid again.

Above him he heard Betty go to the bathroom again.
But it was just an ordinary walk, not the walk he feared.

13

The hotel was impersonal and functional in the American manner and Anne liked it that way. It was built overlooking Bath's Sydney Gardens, and was a ten-minute walk from the centre of the town. She checked in and went up to her room on the third floor. The view was staggering. The hotel also overlooked the lower part of the city. From her window she could see the Georgian terraces on the slope opposite and nearer was the magnificent sweep of Great Poulteney Street. Everywhere she looked were buildings of Bath stone and she wondered, just as she had wondered the first time she had been to Edinburgh and looked across Princes Street to the Mound and the Castle, why she had taken so long to get there.

She tore her eyes away from the window and looked down at the packages on the floor, blenching at the thought of the money she had spent. One nightie had been her ambition, but she had gone crazy, no, not crazy, berserk. What she had in those carrier bags had cost the best part of two hundred pounds, and she felt weak at the very thought.

She had a fast shower and put on a shocking-pink silk chemise and matching bikini pants and bra, and over that a rather more sedate grey skirt and grey blouse. She made up her face with more care than usual. Then she walked down Great Poulteney Street, found the restaurant where she was to meet Tom. She was ten minutes early and went to the promenade next to the bridge and tried to get a grip on herself.

The excitement had begun the moment she had gone into those lingerie shops and it was still with her. But this was no longer the excitement of new clothes, it was a more primitive feeling and one which she had not had for a long time. She had never had it with Clive and what made it even more exciting was that this part of Bath, with the Avon running below her and cascading over the weir, and the buildings golden in the sunshine and the sky filled with fluffy good-weather clouds, this whole scene made Bath seem to be more of a film set than a city, with everyone, including herself, acting out their parts.

But what was she acting in? A variation on *Brief Encounter*? No, that had ultimately been sad. No, this was a new film entirely. She was going to meet her lover . . . well, not her lover yet, but not her boss either. There was no 'boss' in this scenario. Even now, as she thought of Tom, she did not see him against the background of the prison but only in places like his house in the woods and his mother's home in the Wye Valley. She realised that she had lost that feeling of unease with which she had started the day. She almost seemed to be standing outside herself, watching herself.

She knew she was going through a kind of instanta-neous nostalgia of the sort she had not experienced since before Paul's death. And there was another powerful feeling in her head: she was looking forward to something again, not simply existing from minute to minute.

She crossed to No 5 Bistro. Tom was sitting at a table by the window; he waved. She noticed that he was wearing a brown herringbone tweed jacket and a blue denim shirt and chinos. She had seen none of them before and guessed he had been shopping too.

'You're looking very beautiful,' he said as she sat down.

'Thank you. You're not looking bad yourself.'

There was a feeling of tension and she suddenly felt shy. 'I think a drink will help, don't you?' he said.

She smiled. 'I'm not on duty and I'm not driving anywhere so, yes, I think that would be lovely.'

He ordered two *punt e mes* and while they were waiting for them to arrive he said, 'Heard anything about problems in the prison service?'

She shook her head.

'As I was leaving the conference, a couple of delegates were talking about some massive cock-up. Something about releasing prisoners too early, apparently. Sounds bad.'

'Tom, would you do me a favour? We've come a long way just so we don't have to be thinking or talking about the service.'

He held up his hand. 'Not another bloody word.'

They had a long lunch of terrine and monkfish casserole

and strawberries and cream. They drank an Australian chardonnay, and it was past three o'clock before they had finished their coffee.

'I can offer you several options,' Tom said. 'We can have a walk round the town and go to the Roman baths. If you've never seem them, they're a must. Or we can get a river boat and go up to Bathford and back. But there's a third option. I put it to you once before but this time it's not coffee or etchings. I've got a bottle of Calvados in my room and we could have a liqueur.'

'You know something?' she said. 'I love Calvados and I haven't had one for a long time.'

They went back to his room. It was a double, with a kingsize bed. He gave her a small glass of Calvados and offered her dark Belgian chocolates. She took one and felt, for the first time, sinful.

She had the chocolate in one hand and the Calvados in the other when he kissed her. As their faces came together she realised that he was holding the same things in the same hands and they kissed with their arms outstretched not touching each other, like children pretending to fly.

'I think we'd better get rid of the comestibles,' he said.

'Yes, I think we'd better.'

They made love on the big bed. At first there was anxiety on both their parts that this should be something good, and because of that it nearly wasn't. It was Anne who realised this. She wasn't relaxed and nor was Tom. So she put her arms tightly round his shoulders, and as she rolled over on top of him she felt his whole body abruptly soften with a kind of plasticity that it had not had before. From that moment everything changed, and she knew that she had experienced nothing like this since Paul. When it was over and they were lying close in each other's arms, she saw over his shoulder that her new pieces of underclothing were lying in a careless tangle on a chair, the chemise crumpled into a little ball. Oh, to hell with it, she thought. Easy come, easy go, and rubbed her fingers very gently up and down his chest.

Watch drove the big old Rover through the Kingstown streets. He was not the fastest driver in the world and would not have laid claim to be but, more importantly, he might have qualified as one of the safest. He had covered vast distances in Africa at the wheel of Henry Vernon's collection of trucks and rare cars over a period of nearly forty years and had never had an accident. Henry, on the other hand, drove fast, eccentrically, and had had several. So it was with his usual sedateness that he arrived at Hilly's school to pick her up on the last day of the summer term. The kids were slightly later today because there had been a special school lunch with games and singing and a play called *Treacle* which children and staff had made up together and to which no parents were invited.

Watch, like the other parents, sat in his car and waited. The cars formed a line outside the school and the usual practice was for a teacher to stand at the gate and let the kids out one by one. They were then scooped up by their mothers and the street became quietly suburban once more.

This is what happened now. Watch could hear the shrill voices as the boys and girls came rushing out of the buildings. A teacher he didn't recognise unlocked the gate and the kids, shouting and laughing, began to pour out onto the pavement. Watch saw to it that the passenger door was unlocked. He usually kept all the car doors locked because on a trip he had taken to Johannesburg before he came to Britain, he had been robbed when his car was stopped at traffic lights. The back door had been ripped open and an overcoat which he had had for twenty years and which he loved, had been taken. It had happened fast, between the lights changing from red to green.

The flow of children became a trickle then stopped. The cars left. In a few moments he found himself alone in the road. The teacher made preparations for leaving and he hurriedly got out of the car. 'Please do not lock the gate,' he said. 'I'm still waiting.'

The woman was young, not much more than a girl in Watch's eyes. She looked at him expectantly. 'Do you want something?' she said.

'I am waiting for a child.'

'You've come to pick someone up?'

'That is right. Hilary Vernon.'

'Do we know you? I mean, have you permission?'

Watch's heart sank. The whole process of identification and the finding of the letter giving him permission was all going to start again. He said, abruptly, 'Please ask your superior. My name is Mr Malopo.'

A flicker of annoyance crossed her face. 'Who did you say you were waiting for?'

'Hilary Vernon.'

'Which class?'

'She is in Miss . . .' He remembered that Miss Jennings was in hospital but could not remember the name of the teacher who was substituting for her. 'I cannot remember her name.'

'I see.' The way she said it made Watch feel that this was the final straw.

'Please ask. There is a letter about me in Miss Jennings's eh-filing cabinet.'

'Her what?'

'Eh-filing cabinet.'

She frowned. 'Just wait here, please.'

Watch waited.

In a few moments the young teacher was back, now with the headmistress. Watch hadn't met her but that was soon put right.

'Mr Malopo,' she said, putting out a hand. 'I'm Marjorie Strickland.' She was large and comfortable and somewhat untidy. Watch approved of her. She looked like his idea of what a woman should look like. Her hair was reddish-brown, shot through with silver.

'You're waiting for Hilary Vernon, is that right?'

'That is right. There is a letter to say I can collect her.'

'Oh yes, I know all about that. Miss Jennings has it. I saw it when it first came from Hilary's mother. Her grandfather picks her up too, doesn't he?' She didn't wait for an answer but turned to the young teacher and said,

'Harriet, I wonder if she's got locked in the loo.' To Watch she said, 'They go to the staff lavatories sometimes. They shouldn't but they do. And they've got locks on them. Harriet will go and look while we glance in the classrooms. Won't you come with me?'

But Hilly wasn't in the staff lavatories and she wasn't in the classrooms and Watch went with Mrs Strickland to her office and she said, 'I'll just phone Miss Garth, she's looking after Miss Jennings's class while she's in hospital. You heard about Miss Jennings?'

'I heard.'

Mrs Strickland was thumbing through an address book. 'Ah, here it is.' She dialled and listened for nearly a minute and then put the phone down. 'Mr Malopo, we have a little problem here. It's possible that Miss Garth may know where Hilary is but Miss Garth was going to Scotland today. She asked if she could leave at lunchtime – there was only the singing and the games and the play after lunch. So I said, of course she could. The point is, she may have left already or she may be doing some last-minute shopping and driving up during the night. I can only keep on trying.'

'The police must know.'

'Of course they must, but first I'll go round to Miss Garth's flat. She usually leaves a key with her neighbour, or she has in the past anyway, and then we'll know.' She rose and began collecting things and putting them into a large shoulder bag. 'In the meantime I'm going to get a couple of staff members to search through the school from top to bottom. Why don't you just go back home

and check that she isn't there? There may be some reason
we don't know. She might have been picked up early by
her mother or by her grandfather.'

'I thought of that.' There was a slight hint of contempt in Watch's voice. 'She is in eh-Bath.'

'Her bath?'

'West-of-England-Bath . . . at a conference.'

'Oh, that Bath. Well, let's not worry her just yet. Why
don't we do what I've said first?'

Watch went back to the car. He looked on the floor at
the back, just in case. But Hilly wasn't there. The same
applied to the house. He started calling her name the
moment he unlocked the front door. Then he went down
into the garden. Nothing. He got back into the car and
drove to the centre of Kingstown, parked it on a double
yellow line, something he would never have done under
normal circumstances, and went into the offices of
Bannister, Burleigh & Bleache.

'Mr Vernon?' said Miss Moberly to Watch. 'I'm afraid
he's busy at the moment. Can I help you?'

Watch could see, past Miss Moberly's desk, the short
powerful figure of the Judge at the end of a blocked-off
passageway. He was standing with his back to them and
working a photocopying machine.

'I must see him,' Watch said.

'Yes, well, I'm afraid that isn't possible.'

Watch had stopped listening to her and walked past
reception. 'Judge.'

Henry turned quickly. He saw Watch and his face
flushed with embarrassment. 'What are you doing
here?'

Miss Moberly arrived. 'I told this gentleman he was not to disturb you.'

'Hang on,' Henry said. 'He's a friend of mine.'

'I know, but—'

'I'll be the judge of whether I want to be disturbed or not,' Henry said.

Watch said, 'I must speak with you.'

'All right.' He turned to Miss Moberly. 'This is private.'

'This is what?' a voice said. It was Mr Baker and he was standing in his office doorway. 'What's all this about?'

'I told this gentleman that he couldn't see Vernon at the moment,' Miss Moberly said. 'And he didn't pay the slightest attention.'

The sound of Henry Vernon's surname being used without a title shocked Watch to the point of drawing in a loud sibilant breath.

Henry said to Watch, 'I'll come out with you. We obviously can't talk in here. Is it important? Must be, otherwise you wouldn't have come.'

Baker said, 'I don't think you'll be going anywhere. Certainly not out of this building for a walkabout with your friend. This is office time and I asked for those copies. ASAP. Now let's get—'

Henry paid not the slightest attention to him. Instead he put on his alpaca jacket and said to watch, 'Come on then.'

'Hang on!' Baker said. 'Just who the hell do you think you are?'

Henry said, 'If I told you, you wouldn't understand.'

Miss Moberly had a rictus grin on her face as she watched the by-play.

Henry and Watch moved past her. Baker said, 'I'm not having this. I'm not having—'

Henry took his panama hat from the hatstand. He said to Miss Moberly, 'I won't be coming back. Tell him that.'

He and Watch got down onto the pavement and Henry said, 'Before you get the wrong idea, let me say one—'

Watch shook his head impatiently. 'I see nothing. I hear nothing.' Then he told Henry about Hilary being missing.

Anne had read several times that it was wrong to equate love with sex. She agreed – but only partly. She had never been a prude, nor had she been a one-night-stand lady either. She had always dreaded the thought of waking up in the morning and seeing a figure in her bed she couldn't put a name to. So sex had something to do with love in her life, or probably the other way round. She had been fond of Clive but never in love with him, but that hadn't made any difference to her having sex with him. Sometimes it had even been quite good. But the operative word was *quite*. With Paul it had been plain good and now, as she walked along the Avon with Tom in the early Friday evening quiet, she knew that it had been good with him and could be even better. Just being with him was causing her to feel an excitement she had not felt for a long time. As they walked, they were holding hands – and she hadn't done that for a long time either.

'Isn't it lovely?' he said, looking across the river gardens to the Cathedral.

They went up on the bridge and leaned on the parapet, and she thought that the last time she had done something like this was with Paul in Paris. There was no feeling of nostalgia, and that was new.

'It's a different world,' she said. And then, 'Which reminds me – I seem to have forgotten everything in Kingstown. I'd better ring.' She switched on her digital phone and it rang immediately. 'There's a message,' she said. She dialled 121 and listened for a moment and then frowned. 'It's from my father – he wants me to call Hilly's school. I hope nothing's wrong.' She dug out her address book and looked up the number. 'Hilly should be home by now.'

She dialled and Tom watched her. He heard her identify herself and then say: 'My father? What's he doing there? Yes, yes, all right, I'll speak to him.' Tom saw her face begin to go grey. She was saying, 'No, of course I haven't got her! Watch was supposed to pick her up . . . Oh God . . . No, no . . . Yes, in Bath, but I'll come right away. And the police? All right, yes, you've checked at the house? And she couldn't have gone home with anyone – one of her friends? Let me speak to Mrs Strickland.' She spoke to the headmistress for a few moments then ended with: 'I'll be there in less than two hours.' She turned to him and he saw tears in her eyes. 'Hilly's missing.'

'Oh Christ. Look, you get going. I'll pack your things and settle up at the hotel and then I'll wait for you at your house. And listen, these things happen, and they're mostly communications breakdowns. She's probably with a friend.'

Anne nodded. 'They haven't been able to get in touch with everyone in the class, so that's what I keep telling myself.' She began to run back along the road towards the hotel.

14

The headmistress said, 'This is Detective Inspector Merrow. He's with the Regional Crime Squad.'

Anne saw a large man in his early forties in a tweed jacket and grey trousers, wearing a white shirt and tie.

'And this is Detective Sergeant Robertson.'

She saw a smaller, younger man, already bald, wearing a brown leather bomber jacket and dark green trousers.

The room was full of people, the two policemen, the headmistress, Anne's father, Watch, and a younger woman she had not met before. Their faces and voices were around her and they seemed to be talking to her all at once. For a moment the reaction to the fast drive from Bath to Kingstown set in and she felt giddy. Then she recovered.

'Any news?' she said.

Mrs Strickland said, 'I'm afraid not.'

'You mean nothing at all!'

Detective Inspector Merrow said, 'It's early days, Doctor. We're only just organising the search.' He had short flaxen hair and reddish sideburns, a fair skin with freckles, and pale blue eyes.

'The search?' She turned to the headmistress. 'But my father said on the phone that you had already searched the school. I don't understand.'

Henry had come to stand with her and he had his hand on her arm. 'This will be much more thorough,' he said.

The Chief Inspector said, 'That's right, Doctor – dogs, specialists, that sort of thing. Take a little bit of time to organise. Won't you sit down? It might be better if we all sat down.'

Chairs had been brought into the room and Anne realised they had been waiting for her to arrive. She sat down and Merrow said, 'We haven't gone into detail yet because we knew you'd want to be part of it, Doctor, and it would save time not repeating things. Now I want to see if I've got things straight.' He looked down at his notebook and said, 'The first time anyone knew something was wrong was when this gentleman,' he looked at Watch, 'said that the little girl hadn't come out with the other children. That's correct, isn't it?'

'That is eh-correct.'

'And this lady here,' he turned to the young woman Anne hadn't seen before, 'Miss Little, you were on duty.'

'At the gate,' Harriet Little said.

'We always have a member of staff at the gate when the children finish school,' Marjorie Strickland said. 'No one is allowed to go out into the street without a parent or a parent substitute to go to.'

Anne broke in, 'Do we have to go into all this? I mean, isn't there something we could be doing?'

'Doctor, you'll have to bear with us,' Merrow said.

'One of the worst things that can happen in cases like this is where someone knows something the others don't know. Communications can get fouled up. I know it takes time and may even seem like wasting time but it makes everything quicker in the end. Right, it's this young lady's job, or was today, to see that the kids got to their right parent—'

'Or parent substitute,' said Mrs Strickland.

'Or parent substitute. For our little girl—'

Anne broke in, 'Shall we call her by her real name? It's Hilary.'

'Right. Fine. Hilary. And her parent substitute is Mr Malopo here. Anyway, you were waiting in your car, and nobody came, and that's the first time anyone had a clue that the little . . . that Hilary was missing.'

'That's what I don't understand!' Anne exploded. 'How could you *not* know she was missing? There was a whole morning and part of the afternoon for someone to notice.'

Mrs Strickland flushed slightly. 'We take a roll call of each class in the mornings. We don't take roll calls every hour.'

'I realise that,' Anne said, 'but surely someone must have known she wasn't here? I mean, we don't even know whether she was gone in the morning or in the afternoon, do we?'

'I'm afraid we don't. The last day of term is always slightly confused,' Mrs Strickland said. 'There are no formal classes, just games and a play.'

'Hilary wasn't in the play. She told me she wasn't.'

'That's right. We couldn't have everyone in the play.

Anyway, she didn't want to be. We asked her and she said she wanted to be a theatre critic. So that meant she was in the audience.'

'That was my doing, I think,' Henry said. 'I told her about theatre critics.'

'Yes, she said she was going to write something. It might have been better if she had been in the play, then we'd have noticed her absence sooner.'

Anne said, 'But what about her friends? They must have known she wasn't there, or at least remember when she was last seen.'

'All her friends were in the play. They were rehearsing most of the morning. It was only our little put-together thing, you know. It was called *Treacle* and we'd only made it up the day before. It was about a pot of treacle that—'

'I think we'd better get on,' said Merrow.

Mrs Strickland said, 'I just don't want anybody to get the impression that we don't take care of our children. We do! The utmost!'

'Ma'am, no one's saying—'

Anne broke in again. 'What about her form teacher? She'd know. Why haven't we got her here?'

Merrow said, 'I'm just coming to that. Let me see if I've got this right. Lady called Miss Garth. Used to teach here before she retired.' He turned to Marjorie Strickland. 'You said she could go before lunch – that is, *before* the play – so she could drive to her sister's house in Edinburgh where she is spending part of the holidays. You don't know the sister's married name. Is all that OK?'

Mrs Strickland nodded. 'Yes. You see, there's nothing much to do on the last day and she wasn't really involved in the play or the games. I mean, she wasn't the real form teacher and was only there because Miss Jennings has had an accident. So I said of course she could go.'

'And you phoned her flat but she wasn't there?'

'Three times.'

'So she could have already gone by lunchtime or soon after?'

'I went round to see her neighbour. Miss Garth usually leaves a key with her, but she did that last night. And the neighbour doesn't know any more than we do.'

Sergeant Robertson said, 'Ma'am, do you know what car she drives and the number?'

'No. It's small and red but that's about all I know.'

Merrow said, 'We can get the registration number from the vehicle licensing people. We've got a computer link. And then we'll put out the word and she'll be watched for on the motorway. We'll also get onto the Edinburgh police and they'll search for the car. Don't worry, we'll find her.'

'But what about now?' Anne said.

There was a noise outside. They could hear a van door being slammed. Anne got up and looked out of the window and saw two men in blue coveralls with German shepherd dogs coming up the drive.

'Dog handlers,' Merrow said. 'Right. We'll start in the attics and work down through every cupboard and every room and down into the basement. And then we'll take the grounds square foot by square foot. There's a lot of rhododendrons and laurel. It's always tricky stuff.' He turned to Anne. 'I've got to ask you this, Doctor, but could she be having us on? I mean, according to your father she's a clever little thing who likes games and stuff like that. This couldn't be a game, could it?'

'God, no. You mean that she'd run off and hide from everyone? No, no. She'd never do anything like that.'

'That's what I thought. Now listen, Doctor, don't worry. We'll find her.'

There were two dog handlers and four uniformed Constables. They had long sticks with them and after they had been up in the attics and down in the basements where the central-heating boilers were, and in and out of every cupboard, they poked their sticks into the rhododendron bushes and the laurel hedges and the piles of leaves and leaf mould, and they poked them into every bush and most shrubs on the place. And the dogs sniffed and ran about and were called and sent off to another area and fondled and they didn't find anything except an old rag doll which had been buried near the hut by the tennis court.

Anne searched too. She and her father and Watch went over the grounds following the police. As she pulled the rhododendron branches aside her mind was engulfed by dread. It had been like that on the drive back. She couldn't remember a single topographic image on that drive; all her thoughts had been on Hilly and where she might be in the school grounds. She had mentally reviewed every corner and pathway and building, at least the ones she knew, trying to place her child in some context. Finally she had come to a kind of scenario. Hilly had been climbing a tree or a wall or something, and had fallen and knocked herself out. Killed herself? No, that image had been thrust out of her mind. She had to be somewhere in the school. That was the scenario.

But the school had been systematically searched without finding her. So what was the scenario now?

Merrow came up to her and said, 'We'll search all this again tomorrow if we haven't found her, but now I think we should go to your house. You never know, she may have wandered off by herself and be there. I'll come with you in your car if I may. We can talk. Save time.'

Anne wanted to scream. There was no way that Hilly would have 'wandered off'. No way at all. She was basically a well-behaved child. She had spirit but she wasn't naturally disobedient, and wandering away from school was absolutely forbidden. In any case she couldn't get out of the gate and there was a fence all round the school.

In the car driving to her house Merrow said, 'Can I just check a few things with you, Doctor?'

'Go ahead.'

'You were away in Bath, is that right?'

'Yes.'

'Important?'

'Well, yes. I was at a conference.'

'Must have been important. I get put in the dog house if I don't go to my daughter's school plays.'

'She wasn't in the play, and it was only for children and staff anyway. You heard what happened.'

'Yes, of course. I didn't mean anything. It just reminded me of . . . well, you know. How things go . . .'

151

The whole of the Bath episode was something else that Anne was forcing from her mind but it was appallingly difficult. She could not get the image from her mind of Tom and herself, both naked in his bed, with Tom on top of her, she on top of him. And at that very moment perhaps, Hilly falling from wherever it was she had fallen from. Or Hilly near the fence. Near the gate. A hand coming through. Sweets. A grab.

Merrow said, 'I have to ask you about the bl— about Mr Malopo. I mean, it's odd, isn't it?'

'What's odd?'

'Well, him going to fetch your daughter.'

Anne, on a knife-edge, was suddenly enraged. 'You mean because he's black?'

'Well, I mean, we don't get many black people in Kingstown. It's just odd.'

'We don't think it's odd. Mr Malopo worked with my father for nearly forty years in Africa. He's as much part of the family as Hilary or me.'

'Right. Fine. Best to clear that up.'

Watch and her father were already at the house when they got there. And so was Tom. He came over to her.

'Nothing,' she said. She introduced him to Merrow. 'This is Dr Melville. He was at the conference with me when I got the news.'

This was only the beginning, she thought. The lies would be coming thick and fast.

Tom said, 'I went to fetch Dr Vernon's belongings. She came as fast as she could.'

'Right. Let's go in then.' Merrow stopped her in the sitting room. 'Being a doctor, you'll have an answerphone.'

'God, yes! I should have thought of that. Hilly may have phoned.'

She ran upstairs followed by Merrow. Robertson was in the garden with a dog handler. Through the window she saw the lights of their torches. Then the light on the machine. There was a message!

'Let's hear it,' Merrow said. Anne felt her heart thudding in her chest.

There was the usual hiss and scratchy noise then a woman's voice said, 'Dr Vernon, this is Fraser's Bookshop. The children's book you ordered has come in. Thank you.'

Anne felt tears of disappointment fill the sockets round her eyes.

'Well, it was worth a try,' Merrow said.

'What were you expecting?' Anne said. 'The kidnapper?'

'The who?'

'That's what you thought it might be, didn't you?'

This was a word that she had not let into her head.

'Why do you say that, Doctor?'

'It's what you think, don't you?'

'Now hang on a sec. No one's said anything about kidnapping.'

'That's the whole point! I've tried to stop myself thinking about it, and also about another word.'

'What's that?'

'Abduction.'

Merrow waved her to a chair in her own house and they sat facing each other. She could hear her father and Watch below stairs searching his flat. Occasionally she could hear the dog whine in the garden.

'What about abduction?' she said.

He nodded. 'It's a possibility. But not a strong one.'

'Why not? There are probably dozens of paedophiles in Kingstown.'

'The school's security is pretty good. That gate's kept locked. No one can get in that easily.'

'But someone could have got over the fence. Or reached over.'

'Doctor, it's a chain-link fence, six feet high – I measured it. So's the gate. Difficult to get over and impossible to reach over. But say, just say, someone did get over. How the hell is he going to get back with a child in his arms?'

'Someone could have cut a hole in the fence with . . . those plier things.'

'Wire cutters. Yes, someone could have, but didn't. We checked all that.'

Tom came into the room and said to Anne, 'The dog handlers are leaving.'

Anne looked up at him. 'They think she might have been kidnapped, Tom.'

Merrow came in fast. 'No, Doctor, I didn't say that. You were the one who brought that up.'

'Well, what's the alternative? You say she's not been abducted, and—'

'I didn't say she hadn't. I said it would have been nearly impossible for her to be abducted from the school grounds unless someone had a key to the gate.'

'Is that what you think?'

'Please, Doctor, I know it's difficult for you. I can just

about imagine what it's like because I have a little girl of my own, but—'

Anne was crying quietly and Merrow stopped. In a moment she said, 'I'm sorry. I didn't want to break down.'

Tom looked as though he was about to come and put his arms around her, and she found she couldn't look at him. She said very softly, 'Do you think there's a chance she's been kidnapped?'

'There's always a chance of anything,' Merrow said, 'but kidnapping is usually done for money – and a lot of money, at that. You don't fit the profile and anyway, kidnapping isn't really a British crime. More Italian or American.'

Tom said, 'I didn't know there were racial characteristics about kidnapping.'

'There are racial characteristics about a lot of crimes, Doctor. But let's just say there's a chance of kidnapping. Who would it have come from? One of your patients?'

Anne said, 'No, I don't think— Oh God, wait! I think I know. Or at least I can make a guess.'

This was something else she had kept out of her mind, screened by the picture of the school grounds she had formed in her mind. Anything else was too horrible to contemplate. But she couldn't keep it out any longer even though admitting it meant admitting that she, the mother of the missing child, might basically be to blame.

'There's a man called Taplin. Ivor Taplin. He was painting the windows. He gave Hilly an ice cream. He—'

155

'Hang on, Doctor.' Merrow rose and stood in the middle of the room. 'Who is this man Taplin?'

'He was a patient of mine. I was unsympathetic and unkind to him, but he thought just the opposite and—'

'Hang on,' Merrow said again. 'You say he was a patient of yours.' He had his notebook out and was writing.

Anne went on as though he had not spoken, the sentences spilling out. 'He was only released a few days ago and, oh God, I knew I should never have let him, but he wanted to paint the house and I'd been so unsympathetic and—'

'Released?' Merrow said. 'Released from what?'

'From Kingstown Prison. Didn't you know? That's where I work. I'm one of the doctors there.'

'Oh Christ,' Merrow said. 'No one mentioned that. I just presumed you were a regular doctor. I would have asked you hours ago for the names of prisoners who might have had grievances!'

'I thought the headmistress would have told you,' Anne said. 'Or my father. Somebody.'

'We were only interested in Hilary, Doctor. Everybody was only interested in her. No one was thinking of kidnap. She was just lost, that's all. Go on about this man . . .' he looked at his book '. . . this man Taplin.'

She filled him in as quickly as she could, and as she did so she saw Tom's face and knew that what she was saying was so at odds with prison policy that he must be wondering if she had taken leave of her senses.

'. . . So he came and painted the windows. He was never let into the house by himself. There was always someone here. And Hilary wasn't even here except for

156

the first time when he gave her an ice cream.'

'. . . Ice cream,' Merrow said, and wrote it down. 'Why would he do that?'

'I thought it was just a kind thing to do.'

'And now?'

'I don't know.'

Tom said, 'You had a good relationship with him once you'd heard his story. I think you told me.'

'What was he in for?' Merrow said.

'Assaulting his wife.'

'OK.' He wrote that down. 'So he was here for how many days?'

'Four and a bit.'

'And you paid him and he left?'

'That's it.'

'He didn't hang around after that?'

'No. But there was one thing.'

'What's that?'

'He'd always wanted a child and never had one.'

'How do you know that? Did he tell you?'

'He'd mentioned it to me. And his cell mate knew. Taplin must have told him.'

'I've got a problem with this, Doctor.'

'What's that?'

'Men don't steal kids unless it's for money. That's what women do. They steal a child because they haven't got one and because they're mentally disturbed.'

'I think he blamed the failure of his marriage on not having a child. He may have thought he could rehabilitate it if he took Hilary.'

'Do you know where he lives?'

'In Kingstown. The prison will have the address, so will the probation service.'

Merrow nodded and then said, 'This may sound rough, Doctor, but isn't it prison policy that the staff must not have anything to do with prisoners once they're released?'

'Yes,' she said. 'It is.'

He snapped the book shut and called out, 'Mike!'

Robertson came into the room.

Merrow said, 'We've got a name. Let's get moving.'

15

Ronnie Payne was dreaming. He wasn't asleep and his eyes were open but he was dreaming. He was in the South of France. He had never been there but he had seen it often enough in TV movies and he was there now. He was driving a Rolls with the hood down and next to him in the passenger's seat was Doc Vernon, and all she was wearing was a thin dress, no bra, no pants. Ronnie was driving the car with one hand on the wheel, the other on her thigh.

A voice said, 'Payne, you got any snout?'

In his waking dreams Ronnie's fingers had been about to touch pubic hair.

'What you tradin'?' Ronnie said.

'I got chocolate.'

'I don't want no chocolate. You come back when you got something better, know what I mean?'

Ronnie lay back, arms behind his head. He was alone in his cell. After Taplin was released they'd put another prisoner in with him but he'd already been sent to another nick. Someone else was due tomorrow. Ronnie wasn't looking forward to him. The last bastard had snored and coughed and used the toilet half the night. Yobs, that's what most of them were. You couldn't say that about Ivor though. Middle class, through and through.

The point was, he missed Ivor Taplin and that was a new feeling for Ronnie. He couldn't remember missing anyone before except possibly his mother. He'd gone to her funeral. He'd been in Wandsworth Prison then and they'd let him out on compassionate. He'd seen her cremated and for a few moments when the coffin went into the fire he had felt a slight sense of loss, not a very deep sense but enough to know what the feeling must be.

The thing was, he'd shared cells with lots of blokes but they'd all been yobs of one sort or another. You couldn't say that about Ivor. Not the way he talked or ate or slept or washed. Very OK, was Ivor. And the thing Ronnie Payne liked best was the conversations. There was Ronnie telling Ivor about his colourful life, his great exploits as Ivor liked to call them – and they *were* great exploits – and then when he'd impressed Ivor he was prepared to listen to him.

Sometimes he wished Ivor would talk about things other than his house, but that's what he liked to talk about. Seventeen Mulberry Street. Ronnie could see it now in his head. 'Nineteenth century', that's how Ivor had described it. And when Ronnie had said, 'What's that mean?' Taplin had explained: 'It means it's more than a hundred years old and was built to last.'

Pink-washed. Black door. Black window frames. Right, Ivor, I'm coming in. This is me, Ronnie Payne. In the front door. Sitting room on the right as you went in,

160

that's how Ivor had described it. Dining room on the left, and down at the end of the passageway the kitchen. OK, Ivor, I'm coming up the stairs now. Blue carpet with pattern. Yes? Same as sitting room. Not same as dining room. Different pattern. So up we go and there's two bedrooms here and a bathroom. Nice little house. Ivor knew it like the back of his hand. And now Ronnie did too. Christ, he even knew that the tiles in the bathroom were yellow. That's how much Ivor had bloody talked about it.

Still, he missed him. Liked to hear about the house. Liked to think of himself with a house like that. That or a little cottage in the country with a swimming pool. That's what he really wanted.

The bloody point was, it wasn't any fun being in this sodding cell if you couldn't listen to someone tell you things or if you couldn't be telling them yourself. And it was all the fault of that bloody Doc Vernon. She'd got Taplin out, no question, but wouldn't do the same for him. No justice in that. Well, she'd pay for it. Both of them down in the South of France. He with a Roller. She with only a thin dress on. Oh yes, he'd make her pay.

'Payne!'

The door was pushed open.

'I told you,' Ronnie said. 'Not for chocolate.'

'Payne, I want you.'

Ronnie turned in his bunk and saw one of the screws whose name was Beamish. The South of France and Doc Vernon disappeared in a flash.

'You want me? What have I done?'

'Christ knows. Governor wants to see you.'

161

Ronnie felt a rush of guilt and anxiety. 'The Governor? Number One Governor?'

'Number One.'

'What for?'

'He'll tell you. Get your shoes on and tidy yourself up.'

'Listen, Mr Beamish, please, I got to know what he wants.'

'Even if I knew I wouldn't tell you. All I got was the word: Governor wants to see Payne, OK?'

'Mr Beamish, you got it wrong. It was the Doc that wanted to see me. She tells me she wants to see me. It's her idea and—'

'Oh Christ, shut up, Payne, and get those shoes on. I told you I don't know what he wants to see you about, but I hope like hell it's to double your sentence.'

Ronnie got his shoes on and combed his hair and straightened his prison blues.

'Beautiful,' Beamish said. 'Come on.'

They went through B Wing to A Wing and then through the heavy doors at the end into the administrative block. The Governor's office was at the far end in a suite of rooms. As he approached, Ronnie could hear loud voices inside. Oh Jesus, he thought, what have I done?

'Payne, sir,' the screw said.

Ronnie found himself standing in the smallest of the three rooms. He had never been in the Governor's office before and his stomach was churning and sending up bubbles of wind.

Roger Stimson, the Governor of Kingstown Prison,

was of medium height with blue-black hair going grey. He had a major five o'clock shadow and hairy hands. He was dressed now in a blue checked shirt which looked crumpled and his tie was pulled away from his throat as though to give him air. He looked up and saw Beamish and Payne. 'Yes? What it is now?' There was irritation and impatience in his voice and Ronnie thought, Oh Christ, something big's up.

'Ronald Payne, sir. You wanted to see him.'

'Oh yes – Payne – Thank you, Mr Beamish. Close the door, please.'

Beamish left them, closing the door after him.

'Right, Payne,' Stimson said. 'I've got—'

'Sir, can I say something? It wasn't me, sir. She asked to see me. Doc Vernon. She went for me. I mean, I don't want to see no doctors and—'

'Payne, just be silent for a moment. I've got some good news for you.'

'Good news?'

'Well, if I were you I'd consider it good news. You're being released immediately.'

'Released, sir?'

'If I had my way you'd stay in until all the proper arrangements have been made with Social Services and the probation people, but I'm told by the legal department that the sooner you're out the better.'

'Sir, I don't understand—'

'I'll try to explain as best I can.' He picked up a pencil then threw it down in irritation. 'Christ knows why it's happened after all this long time, but it has. Payne, you're in for consecutive.'

163

'Sir?'

'To put it simply: you were sentenced for the burglary in Havant but then you were also sentenced for another one in Portsmouth. Different crimes. And consecutive sentences. You understand what the word consecutive means, don't you?'

'One after the other.'

'Exactly. You serve the first for the burglary in Havant and when you've finished that you serve the one for the Portsmouth job. But what the legal people have just come up with – and I'm talking about our legal people – is that if someone like you is sentenced to two or more periods of imprisonment then the period you spent in prison on remand waiting for your case to come up in court should be deducted from both your sentences, not just one. We've been deducting from just one for the past thirty years. Now suddenly we're told by the legal department that that's all a mistake. We should have deducted the remand period from *both* your sentences. So, Payne, in that case you've served your sentence. More than served it by about two months.'

Ronnie scowled at him. He hadn't understood much of what the Governor had said, but he could see the man was hot and fussed and angry. But even so there was something that Ronnie had felt growing inside him as Stimson talked and now it spurted out.

'I don't want to be released, sir,' he said.

'I don't think you really mean that.'

'Sir, I'm all confused and—'

'We can't keep you – don't you understand that?

You're probably already due for some ex-gratia payment. Not much, of course, but something.'

'Payment, sir?'

'Look, Payne, we've kept you here when we shouldn't have, that's what it amounts to, according to the legal department. So we'll owe you something for that. But I expect you'll have to sue us. The government doesn't like just giving money away.'

The phone on the desk began to ring stridently. Stimson said, 'Get used to the idea, Payne. You've got a touch of gate fever at the moment but it'll go when you leave.' He raised his hand and the interview was over.

By late afternoon of that same day, rumours were spreading through Kingstown Prison like a forest fire. It was said that thousands of prisoners up and down the country had been serving consecutive sentences and were therefore liable for instant release. Besides Ronnie there were said to be three or four more in Kingstown Prison. One of them made a phone call to his father and was told that there was big compensation money being talked about – nearly a hundred quid for each day spent above the new minimum time.

A hundred quid a day! Ronnie began to work things out on the back of an old envelope. The Governor had said that he, Ronnie Payne, had overstayed his sentence by about two months. Call it sixty days. Call it a hundred quid a day. So multiply a hundred by sixty and you got . . . Jesus, that was six thousand quid!

But did he mean that about suing? Ronnie didn't know much about suing people, especially government departments. But a lawyer would. The trouble was, he didn't have a lawyer. Ronnie was what was known as an NFA, a no fixed address bloke. Well, he'd have to find one. Six thousand quid! By late that night he had almost forgotten the feeling of confusion and fright which had come upon him when Stimson had told him he was being released.

It was night and Tom brought the Land Rover to a stop in front of the Cathedral. They had been driving round the city for more than an hour through lighted main thoroughfares and dark little alleys, past closed pubs and restaurants. They had parked the car and walked up the pedestrian precinct to the fountain commemorating the Black Prince, on the steps of which the winos sprawled during the day. There was no one there now, just empty sherry bottles and empty beer cans. They had gone round and round the streets where the school was. Now Tom had pulled up outside the Cathedral. The noise of the engine was so loud that talking had been difficult when he was driving: now silence descended on them.

Anne said, 'Well, what now?'

He said, 'We start again. We don't stop.'

'But she could be anywhere. I mean, she might not even be in Kingstown!'

'All we can do is try. The police are trying. Your father and Watch are sitting by the phone. Something's going to come out of it, you'll see.'

'What? I'm not even sure why we're doing it. I mean they're going to find Taplin, aren't they? And when they find him . . .' She let her voice trail off.

'Don't,' he said.

'The policeman, whatshisname, Merrow. He said the fence was too high to climb over but we've just been to the gate and it's lower.'

'Yes, but it's got spikes on top, and barbed wire.'

'I know, but what if it *was* Taplin and he saw Hilly in the grounds and she came to the gate and he lifted her over.'

'She'd never let him do that. Never.'

'But if he'd said I asked him to fetch her. What if he said I was injured? That I'd been in an accident. That sort of thing.' She paused. 'And there may be other places. I mean, there may be cuts in the fence or places where it sags.'

'But the police went round. They said the fence was in reasonable condition.'

She was leaning against the door and was staring ahead of the window. There was a moon, and one of the Cathedral's flying buttresses was etched against its light. Is there a God? she thought. And does He know where Hilly is?

Suddenly she said, 'It was all my fault.'

'Don't talk nonsense. Whatever's happened had nothing to do with you.'

'Yes, it did. If Taplin's involved then it's my fault. I should never have allowed him near the house.'

'Good Lord, you were only doing a kindness.'

'Don't fudge it. It's the sort of kindness you should never do, not if you work in the prison service. That's one of the things they tell you when you start. Don't mix with prisoners once they're released. Well, I did.'

'You didn't mix. You let him paint some windows. That's not mixing.'

'He bought Hilly an ice cream.'

'OK, he bought her an ice cream. Are you registering what we're saying? Two acts of kindness seem . . . well, not seem . . . but it's just possible that two acts of kindness are the start of something . . .' His voice tailed off.

'Something what?'

'Listen, I didn't mean it to come out like that. The trouble is, almost anything we say seems to make it worse.'

'I know. There's only one thing to say. Where is Hilly and is she OK?'

She began to cry again, the same silent flow of tears, no sobbing, no other sounds at all, just a welling up of liquid in her eye sockets that spilled down her cheeks.

He put his arm around her shoulders but she twisted away. He withdrew, feeling a slight sense of shock which she registered.

'I'm sorry, Tom, but . . .'

'I know.'

'Do you? Do you realise that while we were in bed in Bath, something was happening to Hilly?'

'Yes, I do. Do you imagine I don't think of these things too?'

'I'm sorry.'

They sat in the dark of the car, neither knowing how to continue the conversation. Finally he said, 'What now? You want to go on?'

She shook her head. 'My father's sitting by the phone. I want him to get to bed. There's nothing more we can do tonight. All this . . .' she encompassed with her hand the night, the search '. . . all this was just to kill time, I suppose. Tomorrow we should know something about Taplin.'

16

First the knocking. Then the unlocking.

Ivor Taplin might have been back in the nick.

Bang! Bang! Bang!

He came awake suddenly. It was early morning; he wasn't in the nick but in his own house.

The banging came again.

He got out of bed and put on his dressing gown.

There was a rattle of the letter-box flap.

'I'm coming,' he shouted.

He was aware of Betty standing at the top of the stairs looking down at him.

'Who is it?' she said.

'I don't know.'

He unlocked the front door and took off the chain. There were six men on the pavement outside; one was standing in the mouth of the little alley that led to the back door as though guarding it.

'Yes?'

'You Ivor Taplin?' said a big man with flaxen hair and sideburns.

'Yes.'

'My name's Merrow. Chief Inspector Merrow, Regional Crime Squad.' He held up his warrant card as identification as well as a sheet of paper. 'I have a warrant to search your house.'

'What for? What have I done?'

'Is that your wife?' Merrow pointed to the top of the stairs.

'That's right.'

'Anyone else in the house?'

'Just the two of us.'

Merrow turned to the other detectives. 'Right. Top to bottom. Attics, basement, cupboards, false walls, move any wardrobes, see what's behind them, carpets up and—'

'What are you doing?' Betty Taplin said. She had come down to the bottom of the stairs and was engulfed for a moment as the detectives entered the house.

Merrow said, 'We are looking for a missing girl.'

'Well, she's not here!' Betty said. 'I don't want you going into—' She stopped suddenly and turned on Taplin. 'You haven't got a girl here, have you?'

Taplin said, 'I don't know what anyone's talking about! What girl?'

Merrow seemed not to hear him. He turned to his Sergeant and said, 'Take him to his room and get him dressed.'

'Hang on!' Taplin said. 'What the hell is all this?'

'We want to ask you some questions down at the station. Sergeant Robertson will go with you while you dress. And Taplin . . .' Merrow's voice was cold and harsh. 'Don't argue, please. You're going down if we have to drag you there.'

172

Taplin went and got dressed. He came out of the room followed by Robertson. Betty was standing by the sitting-room door.

'What have you done?' she said.

'Nothing. Not a damned thing.'

'You must have done something or the police wouldn't be here.'

All around them doors were opening and closing, furniture being moved.

There was anger in Betty's eyes, just as there had been the night before. Taplin had come in late and Betty was waiting for him in the kitchen.

'Where have you been?' she had said. 'Where's the food? I left you money! I left you a list!'

Taplin had been drinking. He said, 'I had a meal.'

'You used my money to eat out!'

'My own.'

He put his hand in his pocket, pulled out several five-pound notes and put them on the kitchen table. 'Here's your money.' He had seen the shock and anger then in her eyes. Later, before going to bed, he had searched the crockery cupboard for the knife and taken it outside and thrown it in the dustbin.

Now, as Merrow and Robertson led him to the police car, the same hatred, only magnified, was in Betty's eyes.

Anne lay on her bed, waiting for day to break. She hadn't undressed and was still wearing the same clothes she had worn in Bath, the same shocking pink chemise, the pink bra and mini-pants she had taken off so

willingly for Tom just at the very time that Hilly was . . .
was what?'

She blocked the thought.

Since then she had been waiting . . . and she was still
waiting. She was waiting for a police technician to come
and fix a tape recorder to her telephone in the remote
possibility that whoever had Hilly would ring and say so.
She was waiting for Merrow to phone and give her some
news of what was happening with Taplin. She was
waiting for a call from Tom, not that he could have
anything to say about the case but it had become important for her just to hear his voice.

Waiting . . . waiting . . .

A child. A six-year-old child!

Taplin had wanted a child. He had told her himself
how lucky she was to have Hilly. And Payne had also
spoken about him and his need for kids. The dialogue
came flashing back into her mind.

Payne had said something like, 'He says he's going to
kill her.'

And she had said, 'Who?'

'His wife Betty. 'Cos she ain't giving him any kids.'

And Anne had said, 'Because she wouldn't give him a
baby?'

'Yep,' Ronnie had said. 'That's it.'

The words were seared into her brain. She shivered
with horror. But then she told herself that a person who
wanted a child that badly would hardly *harm* the child,
would he? Of course not! She thought of all the baby
snatches she had read of in the papers, carried out by
childless women who either could not have children or

who needed a child to bolster a failing marriage, and in none of these cases had she read that the child had been harmed in any way. Unhappy, yes. Poorly fed with the wrong foods, yes. But purposely harmed? Never.

But those were women. She had never heard of a man grabbing a child because he wanted to love it. Use it, yes, for . . . She blocked out another thought.

He'd look after her. It stood to reason. He'd hardly risk doing such a thing without making provision for looking after her. Would he take her home? If he had, the police would know by now. Anyway, wouldn't his wife have got in touch with them? What woman would want a kidnapped child brought into the house by her husband? Unless it was the wife who was psychologically damaged and for whom Taplin was supplying a need. What if it was . . . what was her name? – Betty. What if it was she who was desperate for a child. But that made it more likely she'd look after it. Wouldn't she?

There was a different scenario. Just say Taplin wanted a child and Betty didn't. Wouldn't he take Hilly some-where else? And who better than Taplin with his know-ledge of houses and flats and hideaways to find somewhere? Who better than an estate agent?

She had to talk to him. That was the best plan. He had told her he thought she was the only one in the prison who had been kind to him. He had opened up to her. Had told her about being a battered husband when every instinct in him was to keep it quiet, hide it, tuck it away. He hadn't even told the court about it when such a statement might have saved him from a prison term. That's how much he had come to depend on her!

175

Well, couldn't the process be reversed? Couldn't she talk to him? Wouldn't he find her a better person to confide in than some strange police figure with all that such a figure threatened?

She felt she was right about that, it would be safer in every sense. She dialled the Kingstown central police station and asked for Merrow.

'I'm afraid he's not here,' a voice said.

'When will he be back?' She heard a voice shrill with anxiety that she hardly recognised as her own.

'I'm afraid I have no information about that.'

'Tell him Dr Vernon phoned and ask him to call me when he gets back.'

She put down the phone; her hand was shaking so much she could hardly settle it in position.

Where was he? At home in bed? Asleep?

She heard a noise downstairs and guessed it was her father. She went down. Henry was in the kitchen filling the kettle. He looked old and drawn, but when he saw her his face lit up and she knew he was putting every last drop of energy into trying to be as normal as he could. She kissed his cheek, feeling the harsh stubble.

'Coffee?' he said.

'Please.'

'You couldn't sleep, of course. Nor could I.'

'It's the waiting,' she said. 'I've just phoned the station. Merrow's not there. I found myself wondering if he was at home asleep and resenting him.'

'He seemed a reasonably good man,' her father said. 'I don't think he'll be at home. I would think he's probably gone to get Taplin.'

'That's if he's at his house.'

'Yes.'

'That's what the call was about. I was going to ask Merrow if I could talk to Taplin. I mean, he confided in me. Told me things he hadn't told anyone else.'

'The police don't work like that. They do the arresting, they do the questioning.'

'But this is rather different and—'

'Darling, all cases are different. The police know what they're doing. They'll ask if they need help.'

They drank their coffee sitting at the big kitchen table, the table that Hilly always sat at watching the portable TV on the shelf above.

Anne said, 'Taplin wouldn't harm her, would he? I mean, if he wanted a child as much as he seems to, he'd prize her, wouldn't he?'

'Of course.'

'He'd look after her. She'd be what he'd always wanted.'

'Absolutely.'

'It would just be stupid doing anything else after going to so much trouble to get her, wouldn't it?'

'Of course it would.'

There seemed to be nothing more they could say and they sat in silence as the day strengthened around them.

17

Detective Chief Inspector Merrow switched on the tape recorder and identified both himself and Detective Sergeant Robertson and checked time and date. They were in one of the interview rooms at Kingstown Central, a bleak place with a wooden table and three upright chairs. Taplin was sitting in one chair, Merrow was sitting opposite him, and Robertson was leaning against a wall smoking. The tape recorder on the table turned slowly.

Both Merrow and Robertson were looking slightly better than they had when they brought Taplin in. They had slept for three hours and had had a shower and a shave. Taplin, on the other hand, had spent the time in the police cells. Both detectives had coffee mugs in their hands.

'You want a coffee?' Merrow said.

Taplin shook his head. 'All I want is to get out of here.'

'Yes, well, we've got work to do first. You are Ivor Henry Taplin of Seventeen, Mulberry Street in the city of Kingstown?'

'Correct.'

'Right, I've asked you to come here to answer questions in connection with the disappearance of Hilary Vernon, six years of age, who—'

'Hang on! Who?'

Robertson said, 'Oh Christ, come on Taplin, you know bloody well who.'

'Little Hilly? Dr Vernon's little girl?'

'Of course. And don't give us that Oh-my-what-a-surprise stuff!'

'Listen, I—'

'No, Taplin, *you* listen. We're going to start right at the beginning, OK?'

Taplin began nervously to rub his hands together. Merrow said, 'It's easier that way.'

Taplin let his breath out slowly. Then he said, 'What's it matter, you're never going to believe me anyway.'

Merrow said, 'The truth will set you free, Taplin. You're heard that phrase, haven't you?'

'Yes.'

'OK then. The truth. First off, you've just come out of the nick, haven't you? What were you serving?'

'Four years.'

'For?'

'You know bloody well what for.'

Merrow smiled slightly and without looking down tapped a series of files on the table in front of him. 'Says you're a wife-beater. You must have damaged her pretty bad to get four years. Did you?'

'I don't know what—'

Robertson came off the wall and stood to one side of Taplin. ''Course you know!' His voice was hard.

'Well, there was damage to her cheekbone and one eye.'

Merrow said, 'Tell me something, Taplin. You ever done anything like this before?'

'Never.'

'No other trouble with the law?'

'No.'

Robertson said, 'You like beating up women? Turns you on?'

'Listen, can I say something?'

'Why not?' Merrow said.

'I want to save time. Let me just tell you that I would never have done anything to hurt Doc Vernon's child. Or Doc Vernon, for that matter. She was good to me in the nick and—'

Merrow held up his hand. 'Give it a break, Taplin. We'll get to the part where you can say you didn't do it. Meantime, just let me ask the questions, OK?'

'OK, but—'

'For Christ's sake,' Robertson said, 'if you want to tell us the truth, why don't you admit to us you're a paedophile.'

Taplin looked stunned. 'What did you say?'

'You heard.'

Merrow said, 'Hang on a bit, Mike.' Then he turned to Taplin once more and said, 'How was Doc Vernon kind to you?'

Taplin was still confused and frightened at Robertson's accusation and Merrow had to repeat the question. After a moment he said, 'She listened to me.'

'Listened to you saying what?'

181

'Well, things . . .'

'Like?'

'Well, I mean, I told her a lot of intimate details.'

'What sort of details?' Merrow said.

'Personal ones.'

'Don't you understand, Ivor, that we've got to hear these details too. If this is what brought you . . . what's the word – close? – to Doc Vernon, then we've got to know what it was you were talking about.'

Taplin was silent for a few moments and the only noise in the room was the tape recorder and that was very faint. 'Well . . . I don't like to talk about things like this.'

Robertson said, 'Listen, Taplin, either you talk to us now or you go back to the cells and stay there until you decide to co-operate.'

'You can't hold me here,' Taplin said. 'Not without a court order.'

Robertson smiled. The fact that he was a young man and already bald, gave the smile a strange, other-worldly quality. 'You're out on licence, Taplin. You really think anyone cares whether you're here in the police cells or back in the nick? It's one or the other, you know. And the only way you're going to help yourself is if you tell us the truth. Now, what were you saying to Doc Vernon?'

Merrow turned to Robertson and said, 'You go on like that, Mike, and we're going to have to change the tape.' He turned back to Taplin. 'Are you going to tell us, Ivor?'

Taplin hesitated then said, 'Well, it had to do with my case and what wasn't brought up in court. My wife

182

attacked me, you see, quite often. Then one day I couldn't stand it any more and I hit her.'

'Attacked you?' Merrow said. 'Your wife?'

'Yes, my wife.'

'But she's only a little thing.'

'I know, but that doesn't make any difference. She attacked me.'

Robertson said, 'So why didn't you tell that to the judge?'

'I didn't like to. Doc Vernon knows it was humiliation.'

'Or bloody lies, Taplin.'

'I knew you'd say that.'

'You trying to pretend you're a battered husband? Let me tell you something, Taplin, we don't believe in battered husbands.'

Merrow came in then and said, 'Well, it's not so much disbelieve, it's just that it takes more to make us believe, if you see what I mean. Proof.'

'Doc Vernon believed me.'

'You told her in detail?'

'Some.'

'And she said, poor old Ivor, what a terrible life?' Robertson lit another cigarette and stood behind Merrow. 'Let me tell you something, Taplin, this is the bloody excuse all you wife-beaters use. You say: "She started it." Well, we asked your missus about you. She showed us her eye, Taplin, where you hit her. And she told us about her cheek where you crushed the bone. She said you'd hurt her before but she'd never said anything about it because she was frightened of you. You hear that, Taplin? Your wife lived in fear of you!'

Taplin dropped his eyes and looked at Merrow. 'I told you you weren't going to believe me,' he said.

'Some more coffee?' Henry said to Anne.

'No, thanks. Should I take some to Watch?'

'I'd leave him. He's not asleep, or at least he wasn't a little while ago. Poor old chap is taking it very badly. Keeps on saying it's his fault.'

'How could it be that?'

'Because he was doing the school run and he feels somehow he got things wrong.'

'If anyone got things wrong, it's me. Listen, did you look at the fence at all?'

'At the school? No, the police said they'd done that.'

'Merrow said no one could have reached over for Hilly. I don't believe it. I'm going to have a look myself. I've just been waiting for the light to get good enough.'

'Well, what if he did reach over? How does that help? The police have got Taplin.'

'Yes, but what if Taplin didn't do it; what if someone else did? I just want to see if it's possible.'

'Want me to come with you?'

She shook her head. 'Someone had better be here with Watch, and the police technician is coming to fix the phone so they can listen in.'

'Why don't you leave it a little later then?'

'Don't you understand? It gives me something to do!'

She went out to her car and was putting the key in the door lock when she saw Tom's old Land Rover fifty yards up the street. He was leaning against the steering wheel half-asleep. She walked up to the Land Rover and

184

said, 'Why don't you go home. There's nothing you can do.'

He brushed his long hair back from his forehead. It was a slow movement, not the fast jerky movements she associated with him.

'Where are you going?' he said.

'Up to the school. I want to check the fence.'

'I'll come with you.'

She drove there in the early morning. There was little traffic about and the school was empty, deserted. Somehow she had expected to see police tapes fluttering and Constables on duty. She had to remind herself that Hilly was a missing person. That was all at the moment: no abduction, no kidnap, just a missing person.

The school and its grounds occupied most of a suburban block. She began to work her way round the fence with Tom. The wire was dark-green mesh, the kind that tennis court surrounds are made from. And Merrow was right, it was just over six feet high, for Anne had brought a tape measure and now she measured it. The gate into the school was lower and made of steel with panels of wire. On top of it was a row of spikes and a double strand of barbed wire. No one was going to lean over that barbed wire and pick someone up from the other side.

The two of them walked the length of the fence as it faced the road and it all seemed in good shape. But the school didn't occupy the complete block. At one end was an electricity substation also surrounded by fences. Between the substation and the school land was a footpath.

'Probably an old bridle path,' Tom said, 'dating from the time this suburb was just green fields. Now it's a public footpath and quite well used too.'

'But who would use it?' she said.

'Well, if you lived on the north side of the school and you wanted to get down to the shops this would be a short cut. It doesn't cut off a hell of a lot but it does cut off something.'

She began to walk along it. Again Tom followed. The summer grass was high but the path it outlined was well defined. It was hard earth with a dusty surface and ran between the two fences. Anne was looking carefully at the school fence.

'See that!' she said.

Tom came up to her. Here the bracing wire at the top of the fence was slack and the fence itself had bowed slightly.

Tom said, 'Even so it would be difficult to pick up a child on the other side.'

He pressed on the top of the fence and it bowed further.

'And look there,' Anne pointed at an area of grass that had been trampled down. 'Someone's been here!'

'Let's go on a bit.'

There were several other areas of flattened grass, as though someone had been standing there. The fence was in reasonably good shape.

'I think people have been looking at the kids,' Anne said.

'Maybe.'

'What else? I bet men have been standing here

watching the kids during their play time.'

'But there's nothing on the other side of the fence to bring kids close to the fence. It's not near the games area.'

'Kids don't always want to be in games areas. I'm sure this is where a paedophile would stand, staring. Maybe he even had a camera.'

'Maybe,' Tom repeated. It was as though he did not want to argue with her.

Ronnie Payne wiped his hands on his mattress. His blankets had been folded into squares and his sheets and pillow cases removed. The bed now had no identity. It wasn't his any longer. He could feel his hands sweating again and ran them under a cold tap.

This wasn't how he had ever imagined things. When he had planned what to do on leaving the nick it was on a grand scale: a hired car, a six-pack of strong lager and a carton of 200 fags, and Teresa in the back seat. Teresa – where was she these days? That was all part of his apprehension, his sweating hands. No time to organise, no time to get used to the fact that he was getting out. No, not getting out, being bloody shoved out before he had made any arrangements and before he knew what he was going to do.

Where was Teresa now, he wondered again. Somewhere in Dorset? That's where he had last heard of her. He remembered the flat she'd had in Southsea the last time he'd come out of the nick. Not much but at least it had been somewhere to go.

Where was he going now?

He couldn't go to his mum's place because he didn't have a mum any longer.

He didn't know where Teresa was.

He didn't know where anyone was.

He didn't know what to do.

If only old bloody Taplin was there. Someone to ask; someone to get advice from. But he wasn't either.

A voice at the cell door said, 'Come on, Payne, let's be having you.'

Now he started the formal leave-taking; the collection of belongings he had arrived with, the collection of money, the search, the dressing, this time in his own clothes, the signature in the book that all was correct, that he had been given back what he had brought in. Then it was 'Goodbye, Payne, and don't come back – we don't want to see your evil little face here again.'

And don't forget how bloody lucky he was to be getting out. How lucky he was that the prison service had screwed things up like this.

He stood outside the huge prison doors. The morning sun was warm but he didn't feel it. He was shivering with cold and fear. This is what the screws had always talked about; this was gate fever. What he wanted to do was knock on the gates and get back into his cell, but he knew they wouldn't let him back inside again.

Not unless he'd done something bad.

18

'You've been a naughty boy, Ivor, haven't you?' Merrow said.

'I've been punished for what I did,' Taplin said.

'No, I don't mean that. Something else.'

Robertson, who had been leaning against the wall again, came abruptly off it and stood on Taplin's left side.

'You've been lying to us, Taplin. Beating up your woman is one thing, lying to us is another. You follow me?'

'But when have I been lying?'

The three men had had a break. Taplin had been left in the interview room while Merrow and Robertson had gone out into the squad room and reported to the Chief Superintendent who had overall responsibility for the investigation into the Hilly Vernon disappearance. Now they were back together. Merrow and Robertson seemed to have gathered strength. Taplin seemed to have lost whatever strength he had.

Merrow tapped the files in front of him. The pile had now grown by almost half since they had first

brought Taplin in. To Taplin its growth seemed omi-
nously portentous.

Merrow said, 'I asked you if you'd ever been in trouble
with the law before you were arrested for assaulting your
wife, and what did you say?'

'I said I hadn't.'

'You sure about that, Ivor?'

'Yes.'

'What about Virginia?' He tapped the file in front of
him. 'Virginia Boston? What about her?'

Taplin began to rub his hands again. 'What about
her?' he said.

'You tell us,' Robertson said. 'And then explain why
you lied to us.'

'But I was discharged!' Taplin said. 'They never found
me guilty!'

Merrow said, 'Ivor, the question wasn't whether you
were found guilty or not. The question was, were you
ever in trouble with the law?'

'Yes, but—'

'Hang on. That was the question, and you said no –
right?'

'Yes, but when you say in trouble with the law it
means . . . well . . .'

'Well what?' Robertson broke in. 'Listen, you were
found having intercourse with a fifteen-year-old girl
called Virginia Boston. That's a crime, Taplin. And you
were tried for it.'

'Yes, but I was only eighteen myself and—'

'Doesn't matter what your age was,' Merrow said. 'A
crime's a crime. And you were found up on Kingstown

Hill in that beauty spot up there, and you were having it
off with this little girl who was below the age of consent.
Now, Ivor, tell me: were you ever in trouble with the
law?'

'Well, if you mean was I arrested and then found not
guilty, yes. But that's not what I mean by trouble.'

'Tell us about it.'

'She told me she was seventeen. The judge said he
thought she looked seventeen. If it hadn't been for the
fact that she was a copper's daughter and she'd run away
from home, nothing would have happened. They followed us up to the beauty spot. Her father was there in
the police car. And they shone torches in on us.'

'When you were having it off?'

'Well . . . yes . . . Anyway, what's that got to do with
this case?'

'Aah,' Merrow said. 'Thought we'd get to that, didn't
we, Mike?'

Robertson said, 'You like young girls, don't you,
Taplin? Virginia Boston was one. Any other young girls
you'd like to tell us about?'

'No.'

'No other troubles with the law?'

'No.'

Merrow said, 'Except now, of course. With this other
little one. What's her name – Hilary.'

'I told you—'

Robertson said, 'Why did you buy her an ice cream,
Taplin?'

'I don't know. It just—'

'Seemed a good idea at the time?'

'Yes.'

'Let me tell you something, that's the kind of operating system that all you paedophiles use. Ice creams or sweets or rides in cars. D'you think we don't know that?'

Taplin said, 'But it doesn't have to be that. Can't you just do something for a child without it being thought you want something in return?'

'Not people like you,' Robertson said.

It was then Taplin saw the tape recorder was no longer running. He wondered if it had been off ever since they'd had the break.

'Let's just go over this part, Ivor,' Merrow said. 'You got out of the nick and the first thing you did was go to Doc Vernon's house. Why?'

'I dunno.'

'I'll tell you why,' Robertson said. 'Because you knew she had a little kid. You did know, didn't you?'

'Everyone in the nick knew she had a kid.'

'And you wanted to get close to that kid. You'd got close to the Doc, now you wanted to get close to the kid. What better way than buying her things.'

'It wasn't like that. Oh Christ, why do we go on and on? I told you I would never do anything to hurt Doc Vernon or her kid. Never!'

'Ivor, are you a qualified workman? I mean, I thought you were an estate agent. Now you're fixing people's windows.'

'I've always been a DIY person and I did a lot of work on my own house when I lost my job.'

'So you went round to Doc Vernon's the moment you

got out of the nick and said, "Oh Doc, can't I fix your windows?" '

'No, it wasn't like that. I was just looking round the town, trying to refamiliarise myself with the streets and the houses when I found I was in her street.'

'That's a bit coincidental, isn't it, Ivor?'

'Well, yes, but that's all it was. And I saw them coming home, the whole family and I thought what a nice family, and the following day I was in the street again . . .'

'Another coincidence?' Robertson said.

'I dunno. I don't really know why. I suppose . . . no, I don't know.'

'Suppose what?'

'It's nothing.'

'Come on, Ivor.'

'Well, it's just that my wife was being unpleasant. I mean, I thought we'd get along better than we did. And maybe that kind of sent me out in the direction of Doc Vernon's. Because she'd been good to me.'

'A kind of mother figure,' Merrow said.

'Can't be that,' Robertson said. 'She's younger than Taplin.'

'Oh, right,' Merrow said. 'No mother figure. Or a different sort of mother figure. A mother with a little girl.'

Robertson said, 'So let's stop the bullshit, Taplin. What have you done with her?'

Taplin opened his mouth but no sound came. Then there was a knock on the door of the interview room and a uniformed Sergeant said to Merrow, 'You're wanted on the phone. I wouldn't have interrupted you, but you'll want to take it.'

193

Merrow rose and went out of the room. He said to the Sergeant, 'Who the hell is it?'

'Edinburgh police.'

He spoke on the phone for a few moments and then went back to the interview room and called Robertson out.

'They've found that teacher's car in Edinburgh – Whatshername? – Miss Garth. It's in a place called the Morile Road out near the Braid Hills. You know it?'

'Never heard of it.'

'Well, it's parked in the road but the place is apparently packed with blocks of flats so the Edinburgh boys are going from flat to flat. Could take a couple of hours yet.'

'You feel like going on with Taplin?'

'I think we should bung him back in the cells. Give him time to get really scared.'

Ronnie Payne was leaning against the War Memorial in the Saturday morning sunshine. In his hand he held a can of strong lager. Looming up on his right side was the Cathedral with its grassy close, and ahead of him, across another grassy slope was the river that ran through the lower part of the town. Ronnie liked rivers so long as he wasn't too close to them. When he was a kid his mum had taken him to stretches of water in parks and he had thrown bread to the ducks. He remembered being irritated once when they had turned up their beaks at the sliced white bread. Now he watched another family throwing little pieces of bread to the ducks on the town water.

In the distance he could see a fisherman fly-casting for
trout. He was dressed up in waders and a fishing waist-
coat and one of those hats you only saw in Sherlock
Holmes' films. He was casting the line backwards and
forwards . . . bloody fool. What he wanted to do was
throw handfuls of maggots into the stream and use a
good bait. This business of the artificial fly was just
rubbish.

He lifted the can of lager to his mouth and quaffed
until it was empty. Good stuff. Hadn't had any since he'd
been arrested.

He was feeling better now. Had to admit that. He
hadn't felt as good for a long time. The sun was warm
and the beer was strong – good words for a song, those.

But the day hadn't been all like that. He'd been scared
all right when they threw him out of the nick – that was
how he had thought of it – and scared all the way into
town. He'd walked because he was too frightened to get
on a bus in case people stared at him. And the first thing
he'd looked for when he reached the centre of town was
some place to buy a beer. But the pubs were still closed
and so were the supermarkets.

That had been the worst time. He had slunk around
the streets thinking the coppers were going to pick him
up. There was a moment outside the closed door of an
off-licence when he'd stood looking at the bottles in the
window and was tempted to find a brick and smash the
glass and grab one.

But he hadn't. He'd gone to a supermarket when it
opened and bought a four-pack of lager. Christ, the
price of drink! But from then on things had got better

and he now had only one can left.

He pulled the opener and the beer frothed out. 'Whoops,' he said, and giggled. He lay back against the War Memorial and drank deeply.

His other hand was playing with the money in his pocket. There was still a good amount left. That was the thing about the nick, if you were a no-fixed-abode bloke they gave you more than if you had somewhere to go. But he was going to get an abode, oh yes. A house like bloody Taplin or a country cottage. Six thousand quid – that's what he'd worked out. But the rumours running around the nick had varied between fifteen and thirty thousand. Some blokes were talking a hundred thousand. Compensation, that's what it was. Compensation for unfair imprisonment. Unfair. Wrongful. Just the very words made Ronnie lick his lips. They were words that spelt real money. And then he'd find Teresa and they'd rent a country cottage. Yes, rent, not buy. Buying would come later 'cos he wasn't absolutely and totally sure about the country. Maybe a town would be better. That's where he had always lived, in towns like Kingstown. Well, why not Kingstown? Set himself up. Decent house. Decent stereo. Decent telly. If not Teresa then some other girl. Got to be the way forward.

He drank again and to his astonishment found that the can was empty. A whole four-pack gone and it wasn't even eleven o'clock in the morning yet. He grinned. Better watch himself or he'd be like one of those bloody meths boozers.

Right. Pull yerself together, matey. What's the first thing to do? Find a lawyer, that's the first thing. Find a lawyer and get him to write a letter to the prison service asking for compensation. Right . . .

He pulled himself up on one of the War Memorial angels and dropped the empty can on the steps. His legs were suddenly weak. 'Whoops,' he said.

He knew he had drunk too much on an empty stomach and he went off unsteadily into the alleyway that led from the High Street to the Cathedral. There he found a bakery and bought a Cornish pasty. He went back into the alley and stuffed large pieces of it into his mouth. He stared ahead blankly as he chewed. He was finishing the pasty when his stare focused on a building opposite. He read the sign which said, *Bannister, Burleigh & Bleache.* Then he saw the word *Solicitors.*

He threw the paper bag which had held the Cornish pasty onto the ground and went in. He wanted the first floor. He slipped once and nearly fell. Christ, he thought, I'm pissed.

'Can I help you?' a voice said.

He found himself standing in front of the reception desk. A woman was sitting behind the desk and he assumed that the question had come from her.

'Can I help you?' she repeated.

He looked at the small wooden plaque on her desk.

'Mish Moberly,' he said, releasing a spray of saliva. A look of distaste crossed her face.

'Yes?'

'Little Miss Moberly sat on a tuffet.'

'Is there something you want?' she said coldly.

'Want a lawyer,' Ronnie said.

'May I ask what it's about?'

'May you ... Christ, listen to that ... I want a lawyer!'

'I'm afraid there's no one free at the moment. Why don't you come back next week?'

'I want to see a so-licitor.' He had difficulty with the word.

'I've told you, there's no one free. I suggest you make an appointment.'

'I want to see a bloody lawyer,' Ronnie shouted.

She picked up the phone and whispered into it urgently. A door opened and Mr Baker came into reception.

'What's the problem?' he said, looking at Ronnie.

'I want a lawyer,' Ronnie said.

'What for?'

'They let me out of the nick. They said I been wrongly imprisoned.'

'Who is they?' Baker said.

'The Governor, that's who.'

'OK, that's enough.' Baker took Ronnie by the shoulder.

'You touch me and I'll break your arm,' Ronnie said. 'I'm a black belt in karate.'

'Well, I'm a red belt in ping pong.' Baker forced Ronnie back through the door and onto the stairs. 'You come back here and I'll have the police in a matter of seconds. Now clear off.'

Ronnie stood in the alleyway. He was frowning. This wasn't what was supposed to happen. He felt frightened again. He made his way to the High Street and bought another four-pack of lager and returned to the

War Memorial, only this time there were three down-and-outs drinking strong ale there. He drifted down to the river and lay on the grass. He opened one can and drank. That was much better, he thought. Much bloody better.

19

'The awful thing is that there's no national police register for missing children,' Anne said. 'I mean, it's just hard to imagine.'

The four of them, Anne, her father, Watch, and Tom, were in the kitchen of Anne's house. They all looked exhausted. Anne's face was grey and Watch's black face seemed to have lost some of its pigmentation and gone a bluish colour.

Tom said, 'There's a national missing persons helpline.'

Anne nodded. 'Yes, I know. I'm getting onto them as soon as Merrow calls.' She sipped from her umpteenth cup of coffee that morning. It wasn't noon yet.

She said angrily, 'About a hundred thousand children go missing in Europe every year.'

Her father said, 'Yes, but most turn up. Hilly will—'

'What's "most" supposed to mean? What about the ones that don't? My God, do you realise there's not even any communication between our police forces about missing children!' She crossed to the phone. 'I'm going to ring Merrow right now.'

She picked up the phone noting that the police technician still hadn't come to fix an intercept. She was told that Merrow was not in the station.

'Yes, but has he come in? I phoned before.'

'He came in but left about fifteen minutes ago,' the voice told her.

She put down the phone. 'Would you believe it! He's been and gone!'

'He probably knows what he's doing,' Henry said. 'He seemed all right to me.'

Anne turned away, unwilling to listen to comforting words. She wanted something done! She wanted Hilly to walk in the front door.

As the thought came into her head the doorbell rang.

'Oh God!' she cried, and ran from the kitchen.

But it wasn't Hilly, it was Merrow and Robertson. They followed her into the kitchen. She asked them to sit but Merrow said they'd stand. There was something ominous, it seemed to her, in the way he refused a chair.

'There's been a change in the situation,' he said.

Anne said, 'Oh no!' and buried her face in her hands.

Merrow understood immediately. 'No, no, it's not anything bad. At least, I don't think it is. Might be good.'

'What?'

'You know we talked about Taplin.'

'Yes, of course.'

'Well, when we left you this morning we went round to his house and took him in for questioning. He denied everything as I knew he would. But then during our questioning I had a call from the Edinburgh police. They said they'd found Miss Garth's car. It was in the Morile Road. Do you know the Braid Hills?'

'Slightly.'

'Well, out that way. The area has quite a few blocks of flats apparently, but of course they had no idea where she was because they didn't know her sister's married name. So they've done a flat-to-flat search.'

'And?'

'Oh, they found her. She'd driven all night, got there in the early morning and was just about to go to bed. Anyway, the point is, Doctor, she remembers giving Hilary permission to leave.'

'But why?'

'Because she thought that whoever she was talking to was you.'

'Me!'

'That's it. It was a woman, you see. Not Taplin at all. The woman said, or Miss Garth thought she said – she's somewhat deaf – that she was Hilary's mother. Anyway, the Edinburgh police are taking a statement.'

'You mean you're not going to bring her back here?'

'Can't at the moment. I've spoken to her and got a description, though. It was a small woman with—'

'Hang on,' Anne said, breaking across him. 'Are you telling me that this Miss Garth simply gave Hilly to a woman who came to the school and said she was me?'

'That's as far as I can understand her. She says she remembers clearly but when I questioned her she sounded a little confused. She's quite an elderly woman, apparently.'

'Oh, for God's sake! Why can't I speak to her?'

'Because the Edinburgh police are doing that. If we need her I'll get her down or go up and see her there.' Merrow had been trying to keep his irritation in check; to the others this was obvious, but not to Anne.

She said, 'So that's it then. My daughter is given away to another woman who says she's me.'

'I know how you feel,' Merrow said. 'But you can see how it could happen. Miss Garth was filling in for someone else and it was the last day of term. Kids are often taken away early on the last day and she thought this was just one of those times.'

Anne wanted to smash Merrow in the face but instead got a grip on herself and said, 'Tell me exactly what Miss Garth said.'

'OK.' Merrow looked at his notes. 'She says she was near the gate. She was leaving early herself, actually on her way, when she saw a woman standing there. The woman called to her and said could she have Hilary. Something like, "I've come to pick up Hilary." The way she said it, Miss Garth assumed that an arrangement had been made with the school. I mean, she called her Hilary. It wasn't just as if she was coming for any child. That, of course, would have caused Miss Garth to be suspicious – or at least, that's what she says.'

'Yes, but did this woman actually say she was Hilly's mother?'

'Miss Garth isn't quite sure of that. She might have said that, or she might have said she'd come to pick up her daughter Hilary. The point is Miss Garth just assumed that what was happening had been pre-arranged and that she – the other woman – was you coming for Hilary.'

'Assumed! God, don't we have enough kids going missing from school without people assuming things?'

'Well, we're dealing with a lady who taught at the school in years gone by when security was much more relaxed. I can remember the school when there was no chain-link fencing round it, just a low wall, and no barbed wire on the top of the gate. I'm afraid that's when she dates from. So she was just acting how she would have acted then.'

Anne sat down in one of the upright chairs and said, 'What did she look like?'

'Miss Garth said she thought she was small.'

'Thought. Didn't she see her?'

'Yes, well, that's part of the problem. As I told you, she's not a young woman and she was very tired when I spoke to her. She'd been awake all night driving.'

'I've been awake all night too. All of us have.'

'I'm sorry. I didn't mean anything by that. She said the woman was wearing a black skirt and a white blouse.'

'Millions of women dress like that,' Anne said.

Robertson spoke up. 'One thing she did say was that the woman had that kind of frizzy hair. Dark hair with lots of little waves in it.'

'Crimped,' Anne said.

'Yeah, that's it. Crimped.'

Anne got a sudden thought. 'What about Taplin's wife Betty?'

'What about her?' Merrow said. 'You mean you think she could have snatched Hilary?'

'Why not? Taplin said they'd always wanted a child.

Listen, if they wanted someone like Hilary – and don't forget Taplin gave her an ice cream—'

'We didn't forget that.'

'No, what I mean is he got friendly with her. But he would have known he'd be the first person we'd think of, so what about his wife? They'd be in it together!'

Merrow said, 'That's not the impression I got from their relationship. It sounded as though she hated him.'

'But that could all be part of the plan.'

Robertson said, 'Miss Garth put the woman in her early thirties. Mrs Taplin is in her early forties. Anyway her hair's not crimped.'

'Oh, for God's sake!' Anne burst out. 'Anyone can crimp their hair and you only have to wash it for it to come out.'

Even as she spoke she knew she was becoming irrational and moving further and further along a road that led nowhere. The police were looking at her with impatience. Henry was not meeting her eyes.

Merrow said, 'There was something else. I don't know how valuable it is, but it's worth exploring. Miss Garth seems to remember that the woman had a foreign accent. It was possibly Italian or Spanish. Do you know any Italian or Spanish women? People who may have worked for you in the prison? Wives of prisoners? People you've employed here?'

Anne bit her lips as she thought.

'Or Portuguese perhaps. I'm not sure Miss Garth could tell the difference between a Spanish and a Portuguese accent, and there are quite a few Portuguese women working domestically in Kingstown.'

206

Anne finally shook her head. 'No, I don't know anyone like that.'

Merrow said, 'Well, it was just a thought. She's not sure herself.'

'Oh God!' Anne said. 'If only there'd been a regular teacher on duty, none of this would have happened. Hilly would be here in the house watching TV.' The tears came up then and she fought them and turned away.

Merrow said, 'We'll go and see Mrs Taplin. You never know. I'll ring you.'

At the door Robertson said, 'And there have been no calls? I'm not talking about calls obviously about Hilary, but odd calls, wrong numbers, anything like that – calls that would place you here in the house.'

'Not to me.' She looked at her father. He shook his head.

'Nothing?' Robertson said. Then he opened his mouth to say something more and decided against it.

Merrow said, 'You know, in situations like this we always think the woman is local. And it makes sense now. She knows the school, she knew Hilary's name. They'll probably be somewhere in the city or the sur-roundings.'

'But *where*?' The anxiety in Anne's voice was like an organ chord.

'Look, Doctor, we'll work on the foreign accent aspect,' Merrow promised. 'I'll go back to the school, find out what domestics they've been employing. We'll also check the hospital – they employ quite a few there as cleaners. And all the domestic employment agencies.

Somebody's bound to come up with something.'

Anne stared at him.

'We'll ring you,' Merrow repeated, and then they left.

Ivor Taplin stood at his sitting-room window staring out into Mulberry Street. He was hardly aware of where he was. Since he had come back from the police station he seemed to have had a series of black-outs. He would find himself sitting on the side of his bed, or standing here by this window, not really able to remember how he got there or what he was doing there. After they'd released him from the police station he had simply walked for hours in the town but where he'd been and what he'd seen he had no idea.

His brain felt as though it had been battered, as though he had taken some drug which dampened down some parts while leaving others working.

He had never experienced an interrogation like that. When he'd been arrested for injuring Betty he had simply pleaded guilty and had told his story to the first cop who asked him. There had been almost no interrogation. He had made a statement and signed it and that had been that.

But today there had been moments when he had felt like confessing just so they would stop the questions. Especially Merrow. He knew it was Robertson who was being the hard man, who had been threatening, yet he had not been afraid of him. It was Merrow, with his hairy sideburns and his soft voice and the way he had used the name 'Ivor' that had frightened him. *And* seeing that the tape recorder was switched off. He'd thought then that they were going to take their fists to him.

But they hadn't. Suddenly they had left the room together, and had come back half an hour later and said, 'OK, Taplin, that's it. You can go now.'

There were a lot of things he had wanted to say to them; he had wanted to ask them why they had brought him in, who had told them about him. But it was obvious, wasn't it? Doc Vernon had told them, and that's why they had brought him in. Doc Vernon! The thought that she must have gone to the police and implicated him caused something inside him to shrivel up. He had trusted her; he had told her things he had never told anyone – and now this.

He felt a fluttering panic. She had been like some form of security backstop for him. He could not have described exactly what she would have been able to do for him – nothing, probably – but her presence in the background meant that someone believed in him. She had given him a job of work – the first he had had for years – and had paid him in actual cash.

Well, prison had taught him many things and one of them was that you trusted no one, not Doc Vernon and, when all was said and done, not Betty either. There were times when he had wanted Betty so badly he had almost banged his head against the cell wall. But there were other times when he knew that whatever he did, he was not likely to change her. He had read about battered husbands and battered wives while he was inside. There was a correlation between them – many had been victims of family violence when they were children and he knew this applied to Betty.

She had rarely spoken of it, but when she did he had been able to paint pictures in his mind of what her life had been like. Her father had been a long-distance truck driver, away for weeks at a time on journeys to Turkey and Greece. She and her mother had had some peace then in the council flat in which they lived. But gradually as the time came for him to return, tension had grown between Betty and her mother, so that for a few days just before he got back, Betty was having to keep out of her mother's way – not easy in a small flat – in case she was smacked in the face or hit about the body. For the first few days after her father got back, things were usually all right and the three of them were happy. There were presents and there was money and they went out for meals. But then the flat became like a prison for him. He was so used to the open road, so used to sleeping by himself in hotels or in the bunk behind the driver's seat of the lorry, so used to making decisions which only affected himself, that he gave vent to his frustration in violence. He battered his wife and he battered his daughter – and then he would leave for another three weeks or month and things would settle down until the tension for his return began building up again.

Thinking of it now, Taplin realised that any hopes he might have had while he was in prison for his and Betty's future were built on nothing more than hope itself.

At that moment he heard her key in the lock. He looked at his watch. It was not her time to be in the kitchen yet. He moved quickly so that she would not see him through the open sitting-room door. He heard her go up the stairs. He stood listening. He heard the loo flush. He heard her bedroom door close. He decided, while he had the chance, to make himself a cup of tea before she came down into the kitchen.

He filled the kettle and was just returning it to its stand when he heard a noise. He looked up and she was in the doorway.

'You bastard!' she said. 'You bloody bastard involving me in your dirty crimes.'

'I don't understand, Betty.'

'You don't understand.' She laughed contemptuously and for the first time he noticed that the skin under her injured eye seemed to have sagged inwards, which made the eye appear to be slightly lower than the other one. 'You start fooling around with young kids and I'm the one that gets blamed.'

'I never fooled around with a young kid. They've had me at the station making the same accusations and they've let me go. So that's rubbish.'

'But then they had *me* in. Thought *I* might have been the one to "entice" her – that was their word – out of the school grounds so that she would be ours, yours and mine. My God, as if I'd want to share anything with you! And it was only when I went over my whole day they phoned my clients and found I'd been with them that they let me go.'

'But I never mentioned you to them. It wasn't my fault.'

She stood there, a small woman who had once been pretty and bright and with whom he had thought to live his whole life. Now all he could see was someone filled with hatred for him.

211

'I'm sorry,' he said. 'They won't want us again. You have the kitchen.'

He brushed past her and went into his sitting room.

He saw a shape at the window. Someone was standing in the street, looking in. Whoever it was tapped on the glass. Taplin went to the window and inspected the figure. He recognised him instantly; it was Ronnie Payne.

20

'Ronnie?' Taplin said. 'Is that you?' He had opened the front door.

"Course it's me, who'd you think it was?'

Taplin looked up and down Mulberry Street, expecting to see a police car come hurtling round the lower corner.

'What the hell are you doing here?'

'Come to see you, squire.'

'Jesus, get in.' He held the door for Payne and led him into the sitting room. 'Listen, Ronnie,' he said. 'This is no good. I don't know how the hell you did it but they'll get you, and all your remission for good behaviour will go out the window. You may even get an additional sentence. Give yourself up.'

Ronnie rubbed his acne-scarred cheek. 'What the hell are you talking about? I only just got out – why should I want to go back?' His eyes were bloodshot and he was talking slowly; although he smelled of beer, he had slept off his mini-binge and was sober again. The gate fever of this morning was now a distant memory. Ronnie was carrying a shoulder bag which he dropped wearily to the floor.

Taplin said carefully, 'Ronnie, I'm not going to get involved in this. You escape, that's your business. But I'm only out on licence. They'll make me go back if I help you hide.'

'Oh Christ, you think I knotted the old bedsheets and scarpered? Let me tell you, it ain't like that at all. They *let* me go.'

Taplin was confused. 'Let you go? But you had—'

'That's the best part of it,' Payne said. 'They made a mistake, didn't they, the prison department. Kept me in too long. I got consecutive sentences and they put the time I served on remand against only one when they should have put it against both. Something like that.' He yawned and collapsed onto Taplin's sofa.

Taplin smacked his hands together. 'I read about that in the paper today. So *you* were one of those released.'

'I heard there was another four in the nick what got let out.'

'The paper says they've released more than five hundred people throughout England and Wales. People like you who were serving consecutive sentences. Most of them are pretty hard cases. A lot of them were serving consecutives for violent crimes. You want a drink?' he asked, cheering up suddenly. 'I've got nothing in the house but we could go to a pub.'

'Never say no to a good offer.'

Taplin smiled. 'A bit like old times, Ronnie.'

They walked to a pub in the next street. Taplin was strangely pleased to see someone he had never thought to see or want to see again. He was still jumpy from the police interrogation and angry with Doc Vernon for

214

putting him into a position where he had had to endure it. Ronnie was a shot in the arm. Someone to have a drink with on an evening that had been about to stretch into infinity.

'On me, on me,' Ronnie said, putting a five-pound note on the bar top.

'I'll get the next then.'

Ronnie tapped the five. 'Going to be plenty more where that came from.'

'Oh?'

'Yeah. Thousands. Compensation. Some of the blokes are talking thirty, forty thousand for unjust imprisonment. I'm going to get me a lawyer.'

They toasted freedom and each other and then Taplin said, 'Don't spend it all, Ronnie.'

'What's that supposed to mean?'

'There's a bloody great row started. The government says none of you should have been released. It's the prison service that's done it, you see, and they did it without telling the Home Office. At least, that's what the Home Office says. And the Home Secretary says it's all rubbish about the consecutives and that the remand was always supposed to be only against one. Anyway, there's a meeting tomorrow according to the paper and they say no more are going to be released.'

Ronnie drank and licked his lips. 'What about the blokes who have been released?'

'They say you're safe – that they're not going to make you go back. It's a hell of a prison screw-up, the worst I've ever heard of. I think the whole thing's going to the courts so I'm just warning you, don't spend money you haven't got and maybe never will get.'

'We'll see about that. I'll find me a lawyer. See what he can do. Anyway, I'm not going back.' Then he said grandly, 'They're not going to make me do anything I don't want to do.' Then, less grandly, 'Listen, they got to pay something, don't they? Can't imprison people without reason.'

They talked for a couple of hours, reminding each other of things that had happened in their shared memories of prison, and suddenly Taplin did not want the evening to end.

'You got a place to sleep, Ronnie? Because if you haven't, you can kip on my sofa.'

That was agreed and the two of them had a meal in the pub and then went back to Mulberry Street.

Less than a mile away, Anne and Tom in the Land Rover were driving aimlessly round the city. Anne had spent most of the day either in her car or in Tom's. She had simply been incapable of sitting at home waiting. They turned into the town centre for the third time in less than an hour. It was dusk now and the streets were filling with people out for the evening. The pubs were all lit up and the restaurants were doing brisk trade. People were still strolling in the Cathedral Close. It was a lovely summer's evening.

Tom pulled into a parking space and switched off the engine. He put his arm around her shoulders. 'Listen,' he said. 'You can't go on like this. You'll wreck yourself and then when Hilly's found you'll find it hard to cope.'

'But will she ever be found?' Some of the hardness which had manifested itself in irritation and aggressiveness had crumbled in the strain and her voice, for the first time, sounded miserable and defeated.

'We've got to believe she will.'

The word 'we' struck home and she laid her head against his shoulder.

He said, 'I'm going to take you home. Have you got any Mogadon?'

'I'm not taking tablets.'

'OK, but I really think this is becoming pointless.'

'But you never know. She might escape from whoever it was who took her. Or the person might release her. I don't want her wandering the city at night.'

'You don't know any of this for a fact. And you don't even know where she might be released. I know why you're doing it – subconsciously anyway. You've got to fill in time.'

She ignored him and said, 'I keep on going over what that teacher said. I can see Miss Garth coming towards the gate, leaving early, and I can see the woman standing by the gate or getting out of a car, and then saying something about coming for her daughter or coming for Hilly, whatever it was, and that bloody woman just going and getting Hilly and handing her over. That's what makes me want to shout out. That's what I can't understand, how Hilly—' She suddenly checked. 'Oh Lord, Tom!'

He waited, seeing her hands begin to tremble.

She said, 'It's something I should have thought of before except I'm so damned confused and tired I can't think straight. Look, the point is, Hilly would never, never have gone with a stranger—'

He covered her hands with his. 'The police went over that, my darling. They said it was quite possible the woman pretended she had a message from you, or something like that. Don't you remember? They told us these people say the most plausible things. What if she'd told Hilly you'd been in a car accident and that she was from the hospital or the Social Services and she'd been sent to bring her to you?'

She nodded. 'Yes, I know that. But I've warned Hilly over and over about that sort of thing: people who offer sweets or rides in cars or pieces of unexpected news that mean she has to go with them. I've told her that if that ever happened, she was to go to a teacher and ask her to phone and make sure. Anyway, the teachers would do that automatically.'

'Yes, but that's if everything goes perfectly and if you don't have a substitute teacher who's in a hurry and wants to get away on her own holiday.'

'For God's sake, stop playing devil's advocate and listen! Let's just say that it did work, that Hilly remembered what we had agreed but didn't carry it through. One then has to ask *why* she didn't do it.'

'All right, why?'

'Because *she knew the woman* – that's why.'

Anne had twisted round in the car seat to face Tom and was pressing her fingernails into the skin of his arm.

'Knew her?'

'Yes. And Tom, who speaks with a foreign accent who is known to Hilly?'

'Anne, I just don't know. She may know more than –
Wait a second! Are you suggesting who I think you are?
Steffie?'

She nodded. 'Think about it.'

'My God! I can't imagine—'

'Tom, she was jealous of what she thought was going
on between us even though nothing was. I never told you
in any detail about a phone call I had from her. She
phoned me one night at home.'

The French-accented voice had come as a shock to
Anne, but it was soft and friendly.

'What can I do for you?' Anne had said.

There had been a dry gurgle of laughter. 'All doctors
are the same. Tom used to say the same thing.'

Anne had tried to get away then by saying she was
putting Hilly to bed, but Stephanie went on: 'We never
had a child. The time was never correct. You know
something? Tom does not like children. He did not want
one. I said to him, "What is marriage without children?"
So you are lucky to have a child. No one can take that
away from you.'

Now Tom, listening in the car, said, 'But I was the one
who did want children.'

Anne said, 'I haven't told you half of it. I've never
wanted to. She said flatly that she wanted you back, that
she wanted to be made pregnant by you. I remember her
saying she wanted to be part of a family again.'

'Steffie always wanted what other people had, and
then when she had it she found something else to want.'

'When I told her there was nothing I could do for her,
she said there was something, and when I asked what it

219

was, she said I could take my hands off you. I told her I'd had enough and I was going to hang up, and she said – and I remember the words perfectly – "Don't hang up, you bitch! I am in Kingstown. If you hang up I shall come to your house. I know where you live".' Anne paused and said, 'I felt sick when she said that. Sick, and frightened too.'

'God, I'm sorry! I had no idea.'

'The only way I could deal with her was to threaten her with the police.'

'Let's just keep to the main track for the moment—'

'Hang on, let me finish. It wasn't too long after that, that she tried – perhaps not terribly hard – to kill herself. You had to go to the hospital, remember.'

'She'd done that once or twice before and there were always threats of suicide. But although I know it all sounds as though she's a possible candidate, it doesn't explain Hilly going with her. Did Hilly even know her? Did they ever meet?'

'That happened one day out at your place. Hilly and I had gone there to see you, Hilly had been playing with the dachsie when Stephanie arrived. Then I suddenly missed Hilly . . .'

Like most mothers she had been listening subconsciously to Hilly shouting. Suddenly she realised she wasn't hearing her any longer. She rose and went to the window. Hilly and Beanie usually played on the verandah or just down the steps in front of it. They weren't there. She craned one way then the other and saw a small car parked at the far corner of the house. Hilly was

220

standing at the driver's window.

'Someone's here,' Anne said to Tom.

He'd gone to the door and looked out. 'Oh Christ, it's Steffie.'

Anne was about to run but stopped herself and walked quickly along the outside verandah. Tom kept pace with her. Hilly was looking into the car and laughing. Anne could see Stephanie's dark hair and white face smiling from the driver's seat.

Stephanie looked up at them and said, 'Hello there, I've been talking to Hilly. Anne, you've got such a lovely little girl.' She turned to Hilly. 'I told you that, didn't I.'

'Yes,' Hilly said.

'Oh Anne, she *is* lovely. You *are* lucky. Don't you think she's lucky, Tom?'

'Very lucky. What can I do for you?'

'Do?' Stephanie laughed. 'I was in Kingstown, so I came to say hello. And to give you your mother's love.'

Anne stepped forward and lifted Hilly up, then walked back along the verandah. Opposite the front door she put her down. 'We're going now, darling.'

'Why?' Hilly said. 'She's a nice lady.'

Tom caught up with them. 'Please don't go.'

Anne held Hilly with one arm and turned towards him. She said in a soft but biting voice, 'Keep her away from me. And keep her away from Hilly.'

She'd taken Hilly's hand and gone to her car and driven away across the bumpy track towards the main road.

Tom said, 'I remember now. You took Hilly and left. But that was before the rancorous telephone call, wasn't it?'

'No, it was after that, and you'd have thought she had never made it. That's what makes it so damn worrying. You know, I never wanted her near Hilly.'

'OK, but as far as we know she's in France and she left before Hilly went missing. She wrote a letter telling me. I read parts of it to you at the pub.'

'She's a devious woman – you've said so yourself. That could just have been done to put us off. And anyway, don't you remember what Merrow said – that the person who took Hilly was likely to be someone local? I know Stephanie wasn't really local but she'd lived here and knew the town well.'

'Yes, but the woman teacher said she thought the accent was Italian or Spanish.'

'Oh God, we all make mistakes about people's accents. And don't forget she described her as having crimped hair. Stephanie crimps her hair sometimes.'

'That was only what that policeman thought Miss Garth meant.'

'Tom, why are you being like this? You're arguing against everything, every single thing.'

He paused and then nodded. 'I suppose it's because I'm feeling guilty.'

'Of what?'

'Well, if I hadn't become involved with you, none of this might have happened.'

'Look, I'm not going to argue that one. If it was anyone's fault, it was mine. I shouldn't have gone away on the last day of term. So leave that to one side and let's get back to Stephanie. Can you believe what I'm telling you?'

'I suppose so. But you know, Steffie isn't really the person who would want to take Hilly over. She talks and talks about having kids, but that's only because she hasn't had any. She says she wishes now she'd had one or more, but at the time she didn't give a damn.'

'So this is punishing us for who we are and because I've got the child she thinks she should have had.'

'Let's say you're right. In that case they may both be in France by now.'

Anne shook her head. 'I don't think Hilly would have gone with her, not without a fuss. Hilly's too much her own girl. Anyway, Stephanie would know, or at least think, that every airport and port was being watched. And don't forget what Merrow said: local, local, local.'

'But where? She couldn't go to a hotel.'

'Of course not. But what about a holiday flat, or furnished house to let? There must be dozens. I'm going to ring Merrow.'

She dialled the central police station. After a moment she said in exasperation, 'But where is he?' Then: 'For God's sake, this is Dr Vernon. He's investigating the disappearance of my little girl.' She listened for a few moments more, then switched off the mobile. She turned to Tom. 'Gone home. Won't be in until the morning.'

'I suppose he's asleep.'

She chewed her lips for a moment and then nodded to

herself and said, 'Who'd know about the sort of places Stephanie might take her to?'

He thought for a moment and then said, 'God knows.'

'Ivor Taplin would.'

21

Tom said, 'Mulberry Street . . . here is it.' They drove up a short way. 'There's number seventeen.'

Anne said, 'The lights are on.'

Tom brought the Land Rover to a stop. It was now dark. They had had to go to the prison to get Taplin's address and it had taken longer than they had thought.

'Let me go by myself,' Anne suggested. 'Taplin and I have got on well.'

She clambered out of the car and rang the doorbell. The door opened almost instantly and Taplin stood in the light of the hallway.

'Hello, Ivor,' Anne said. 'Could I come in for a moment? I want to ask you something.'

Taplin was taken aback. His face changed from polite enquiry to hostility. But before he could speak, before he could even greet her, Ronnie Payne had come up behind him. He was holding a can of beer and his scarred face was flushed.

'Why, it's Doc Vernon,' he said, staring owlishly into the light. 'Ivor, you sod, what've you been up to?

Evenin', Doc. Or was you coming to see me?' He saw the shocked surprise in her eyes and said, 'No, no, Doc, they released me. It's kosher. Old Taplin here can explain.'

She turned to Taplin and said, 'Could we talk privately, Ivor?'

He paused for a moment then said, 'No, I don't think so.'

It was so unexpected she wasn't sure she had heard correctly. 'Did you say no?'

'That's it, Doc,' Payne said. 'He says no.'

Tom had got out of the car and had come up behind her.

'Christ,' Payne said. 'It's the whole bleedin' medical staff!' He turned to Taplin. 'What you done, squire? Or should I say what you got that's catchin'?' he chuckled and belched loudly

Anne tried to ignore him and kept her eyes on Taplin. 'I came to see if you would help us find my daughter. You know she's missing?'

'Of course I know she's missing,' Taplin said angrily. 'I've been with the police for most of the day. They stuck me in the police cells for hours on end. They nearly took me back to the prison. Oh yes, I know she's missing all right! Only *I* didn't take her.'

'No, of course you didn't.'

Payne said, 'Did she say you did, Ivor?' He indicated Anne.

Taplin said, 'Hang on, Ronnie.'

'Hang on Ronnie?' Payne repeated indignantly and drunkenly. 'Is that—'

226

Tom said to Taplin, 'Can't we talk to you in private? It's vital. We think only someone like you may be able to help.'

Payne said, 'First she gets you out of prison, then she turns you in to the coppers. Some friend.'

Taplin said, 'Ronnie, let me just talk to Dr Vernon in the sitting room for a sec. Why don't you go through to the bedroom – get yourself another beer.'

Payne's eyes lit up and he said, 'Your house, Ivor. You're the boss.'

Taplin took Anne and Tom into the sitting room while Payne fetched another beer from the fridge and drifted into Taplin's bedroom.

Taplin motioned them to seats but stood himself. Anne said, 'I'm very sorry that should have happened to you, Ivor. They had to check.'

'But why check me? All I did was give her an ice cream. They kept on and on about that. Why did I give her an ice cream if I wasn't a paedophile? You see, according to them, only a paedophile would give a little girl an ice cream.'

'I'm desperately sorry,' Anne said.

'For God's sake, one ice cream!'

'It's the times we live in,' she said. 'An act of kindness becomes a crime.'

'And then you said to them: "Taplin's the most likely one to have taken her. Taplin's always wanted a child. Taplin gave her an ice cream." And then when that proves a dud: "What about Taplin's wife?" ' He had been pacing up and down the room and now stopped and turned on her. 'I thought you were my friend. I told you things in prison I'd never told anyone. Not the police. Not even as a mitigating circumstance in court. And then you did that to me.'

Anne had been staring down at her hands and now she looked up at him and said, 'I've told you I'm sorry. That's all I can say. But just imagine if you had had the child you always wanted, and she was a little girl of six, and she disappeared. Suddenly and for no reason, just vanished. What would *you* have done? Wouldn't you have given the police the names of anyone you could think of, even if one of them was your own brother? Wouldn't you have given them his name too?' He stood looking down at her. 'Well?' she said. 'Wouldn't you?'

He shook his head, not to disagree, but as though to clear it. Then he said, 'I trusted you.'

'I know you did, but what can I say? If the same thing happened I'd do exactly the same again.' She indicated Tom and said, 'If I thought Dr Melville could have done it I'd have given the police his name.'

'Well, did you give them that black man's name? It seems he might have been a name to consider.'

This time it was Anne who shook her head. 'You'll just have to believe that Watch is almost as close to me and to Hilly as my own father. It's not possible.'

'Only me, then, is that it? Only Taplin the paedophile? And I don't even know what the police are going to do tomorrow. They may come for me again. And for Betty. They didn't say a bloody thing except: "You can go now, Taplin. We won't be needing you any more today." No explanation, no thanks, no apology.'

228

There was a slight pause as both seemed to have run out of breath and Tom said softly, 'Dr Vernon's apologised as deeply as she can, but remember what she said, Mr Taplin. What if the child was yours?'

It was only the second time Taplin had heard anyone call him mister in a long while, and the word hung there in the sitting room like a symbol. He stopped pacing and stood in front of Anne and after a long moment said unwillingly, 'OK. How can I help?'

She stood up, facing him and said, 'First of all, let me tell you why the police released you. One of the teachers, the one who let Hilly go from the school grounds, says she passed her over to a woman she thought was me.'

'Thought she was you?'

'Her mother. And we think we know who this woman is. We're guessing but we think we do. And because the police have said it several times, we think they may still be in Kingstown. We think she might have taken Hilly to a rented flat or house or holiday apartment, and we thought that with your expertise you might be able to guide us.'

'Guide you?'

'Tell us the most likely places they could have gone.'

'But there are dozens of rental flats in Kingstown. And most of the leases are for six months. People don't like letting for less than that.'

'That's why we thought of a holiday flat.'

Taplin said, 'I've been out of the business for too long. I'm no expert now.'

'But don't you know people who are?'

'Well . . . one or two, I suppose.'

'We wondered if you might ring them and ask, you know, if they remember a woman. She is slender and attractive and has dark crimped hair and speaks with a French accent. You could ask if any of them remembered letting a flat to a woman like that. They'd be bound to remember her.'

'I suppose I could ring a couple of old colleagues in the morning.'

'No, not in the morning. Now.'

'But why don't you go to the police? Couldn't they find out?'

'They'd have to come to someone like you, and anyway, our police are off-duty, asleep.'

'The two who questioned me?'

'Yes, those two. Will you?'

He looked at his watch. 'It's a bit late for that, isn't it?'

Sombrely, Tom said, 'Time doesn't come into it. Not when a little girl is in danger.'

'Look,' Taplin said, 'I've just come out of prison. These people know I've been inside . . . it's embarrassing.'

Anne said, 'We're talking about a missing child.'

'Yes, I know.'

'If you won't make it for my sake, then make it for Hilly's.'

He gave a slight shrug then turned and walked over to a side-table on which the telephone stood. From a small drawer he took a Filofax. 'Haven't used this for a long time,' he said.

They sat and watched him. He paged through the

book then stopped and dialled. 'Can I speak to Hugh?' he said. 'Oh hi, it's Ivor Taplin. Yes, Ivor. Oh, the other day. I'm out on licence. Yes, yes, bloody pleased. Listen, Hugh, I'm sorry to ring up so late but it's a matter of urgency. I've been asked to help trace a missing girl. What? Yes, here in Kingstown . . . six years old. Her mother thinks she may have been taken to a holiday flat and is being hidden there. Didn't you have the Cavendish Group's flats on your books? Oh, really. I didn't know that. I'm very out of touch. OK, Hugh, thanks very much.'

He put down the receiver and turned to them. 'Well, that's one non-starter. There used to be a company called Cavendish who had holiday flats but they've been turned into permanent flats for elderly people. So nothing there.'

He consulted his Filofax and this time he spoke to someone called Ralph. He repeated what he had said the first time and talked for five minutes. He put down the receiver and said to them, 'That was another man who handled holiday lets. He says that all his flats are let for the season. Most were booked a year ago. He doesn't remember anyone like the woman you describe.'

Taplin spent the next thirty minutes phoning. Two calls went unanswered. Finally he closed the book and turned to them and said, 'That's it. That's all I can do.'

They had watched him in silence. Anne had hoped and hoped each time he dialled this time he would contact someone who recognised Stephanie's description.

The three of them stared at each other. Then Anne said, 'And that's all of them? I mean, all of the flats that she could have taken?'

'Except for the two agents who didn't answer, but I have to say they never did much in the holiday letting area, anyway. Not when I was working. 'There's just no – hang on, there *was* one other company. In fact, I had it on my books for a time. God, what was his name? Began with an S – no, it didn't a Z. Zanoni – that's it! He owned restaurants and branched out into property in the early eighties when it was the thing to do. He bought some holiday flats out in the suburbs.'

'Where?' Tom said.

'You know the greyhound stadium in Atherton?'

They shook their heads.

'It's out on the Southampton road.'

Anne looked at Tom but he shook his head. 'Don't know that part of town at all.'

'Won't you take us there?' Anne said.

'Maybe tomorrow if you like.'

'No, tonight,' she insisted.

'Now?'

'Look, all you have to do is go in your car and we follow and when you get to the flats you come home and we do the rest.'

'My car! I haven't got a bloody car. Don't you understand, I've been in the nick! And anyway, what about Ronnie? He's looking for somewhere to sleep. I can't just leave him here.'

They didn't try to argue with him or pressure him. They said nothing. They simply stood there, looking at him.

'Oh Christ,' he sighed. Then he walked into his bedroom and they heard him say to Payne, 'I've got to go
out for a little while, Ronnie. There's more beer in the
fridge. Just keep the bedroom door closed.'

'Right, squire. Whatever you say, squire.'

22

'Go left at the next set of traffic lights,' Taplin said. He was sitting in front with Tom so that he could navigate and Anne had gone to the back seat. Since they had left the centre of the city and driven east she had soon become lost. She had never been this way before and nor, she now knew, had Tom. She saw a sign to the railway station and then the road began to rise up a small hill. The houses here were rows of semis built in the twenties and thirties. Slowly they left these streets behind, and as they reached the outskirts of the city the houses improved.

'We're on the Southampton road,' Taplin said. 'The flats should be on our left. There they are.'

It was a three-storey block containing about twenty flats and originally built in the fifties. Tom pulled up.

'There's not a light anywhere,' Anne said.

The flats were set a little way back from the busy road and they were all in darkness. There was a high metal fence round them and, as Tom took the car forward again, they came to a large notice which told them that this was now a site for the building of a new Kingstown supermarket.

Anne had been tense to the point of snapping as they drove here. Now she burst out in anguish. 'Oh God, would you believe it!'

They had spoken very little on the drive from Mulberry Street and now the silence returned. She felt seized by depression and also by a wave of weariness. It was as though nothing, not one single thing, was going in their favour.

At last Taplin spoke. 'Sorry about that.'

They didn't comment. Then Anne said, 'Is that it?'

'I'm afraid it is,' he admitted.

For a second time she seemed to lose her grip on the strength that had kept her going. Tears seemed an easy comfort and she could feel her throat begin to close.

Then Taplin said, 'There's always the old Rosa block, I suppose.'

'What's the old Rosa block?' Anne's ears had pricked up.

'Zanoni was talking about buying it, but I don't know if he ever did because my own troubles started then. The agency was taken over and I lost my job.'

'Where is it? Can we look?'

'It's more or less on the way back to town anyway. Go to the next roundabout and take the first right.'

They drove through an older part of Kingstown where there were more trees and finally, past the hospital, they came to a block of flats facing onto a side street. Each flat had a small balcony. Outside a large notice said: *Santa Rosa Holiday Apartments.*

'It's been done up,' Taplin noted. 'It was pretty run-down a few years ago.'

236

Now the block was gleaming with white paint and shining glass. Lights were on, music came through the open windows. Anne got out of the Land Rover and went up to the big glass doors which closed off the foyer.

Taplin and Tom joined her. Taplin said, 'You can't just go knocking on everyone's door.'

'Can't I?'

'Well, I'll leave you to it.'

Anne tried the glass doors but they were locked. She looked through them to the simple foyer, which contained just a table and chair and a few potted palms. She said, 'There's got to be someone here during the day. The postman would need to get in, so would people delivering things.'

'There'd be a porter,' Taplin said. 'He'd sit at the table. But the glass doors would be open.'

'What about at night?' Anne said. 'What happens if you lose your keys or need a doctor?'

'There should be a notice.'

'What's that on the wall by the lift?'

'It's a notice all right,' Tom said. 'But you'd need binoculars to read it.'

Anne looked at Taplin. 'Wouldn't they have him in the phone book?'

'Who?'

'The porter.'

'Why?'

'Don't they usually?'

'I never dealt with porters outside business hours, just the owners.'

A block away there was a phone box. They could see

the lights. Anne and Tom hurried to it, followed by Taplin.

'God, look at that!' Anne said. The phone book had been vandalised and the pages lay strewn on the floor. But there were still dozens of pages left in the book and this time they were lucky. The back section starting with Q had survived the attack.

She said, 'Santa Rosa . . . Santa Rosa . . . Here it is!' And underneath the entry was the one she wanted. *Porter. 42, Tanner St.*

'Where's Tanner Street?' she asked Taplin urgently.

'You're standing in it.'

Number 42 was only a stone's throw from the Santa Rosa Apartments. It was a small brick building containing offices. *Zanoni Leases Ltd* stated the lettering on the windows, followed by a list of properties owned by the company, of which the Santa Rosa Holiday Apartments was one. There was a second, smaller door on which a brass plaque announced: *H. Slatter, Porter.*

Anne pressed the bell. Nothing happened. She pressed again. They heard footsteps then the door swung open. A voice said, 'You're late, George, and the little sod's playing up.'

This was said before the door was fully open. When it did open Anne saw a short, plump, middle-aged man with a camera in one hand and a pair of spectacles in the other. Immediately behind him was a staircase leading to an apartment on the first floor.

'Oh,' he said, and put on his spectacles. 'Who are you?'

Anne said, 'You're the porter for the Santa Rosa block, aren't you?'

Slatter looked at her with undisguised impatience. 'Yes.'

'I want to find out if a friend registered to spend a holiday there.'

'You what? I mean, I'm off-duty, you know. It's night-time. It's – Christ, it's late. And you come here and knock on my d—'

'Honk!' a young voice shouted. 'What you doing, Honk?'

Anne looked up and saw a small boy of about nine of the landing. He was completely naked and covered in what looked like sun-tan oil.

Slatter shouted, 'You get back, you hear?' Then to Anne: 'My nephew, Rodney.'

Anne said, 'I want to know if a Mrs Melville registered here and if you saw her.'

'Now listen, I don't have the book here and—'

'Honk, you better come up!' the small boy shouted. 'I ain't going to stand around. I'm getting a chill.'

'Go back to your bath, Rodney.'

'I ain't havin' a bieedin' bath.'

Anne said, 'She was a small woman, attractive, and would have come in yesterday or the day befo—'

'No, no, nobody like that.' He put on another pair of spectacles and looked up the staircase. 'You go and put your clothes on, Rodney!'

'Why? You just told me to take them off!'

Slatter turned to Anne. 'I got to go. He's a naughty child and he'll break things.'

Anne felt an upsurge of pity for the boy who was not much older than Hilly and who would, she thought, probably end up somewhere like Kingstown prison when

239

he grew up. Angrily she said, 'Mr Slatter, if you don't listen to me I'm going to call the police and report you as someone taking pornographic photographs of an under-age child.'

'You're mad. That's my sister's boy. He's having a bath and he doesn't like being left.'

'Honk,' said the naked child at the top of the stairs, 'if you don't come and finish the session I'm going. And I got to have my money this time. Geoff says he'll come and pay you a visit if I don't.'

Slatter looked at Anne and the two men standing behind her. 'All right, what woman?'

Anne told him again. He shook his head. 'No, only arrival yesterday was a phone booking who arrived with her child.'

'A little girl?'

He thought for a moment. 'Yeah. Little girl.'

'Fair hair? About six years old?'

'Honk! I'm telling you!'

'Yes,' Slatter said. 'That's them. Number twelve. Took it for a week.'

'I want to call on her,' Anne said.

'Well—'

The naked child came halfway down the staircase. Anne could see a lascivious little face peering at them in the bright lighting. The child said saucily, 'You come to take pictures too?'

Anne said to Slatter, 'They may be asleep. I want you to open the front door.'

'I can't just leave my nephew like that. Anyway, I'm not on duty.'

240

'Mr Slatter – I'll do what I said I'd do.'

Slatter turned to the boy. 'You go upstairs, Rodney. I'll be back in a minute.'

'Fuck you, Honk,' the child shouted. 'I ain't waitin'.'

Slatter led them at a fast pace across the road and opened the big glass doors to the Santa Rosa Apartments. 'Make sure the door's closed when you go.' Then he turned and scuttled back across the road to his flat.

Taplin said, 'I'll wait down here if you don't mind.'

Tom said to Anne, 'I'm coming with you.'

There were four flats on each floor and they took the lift up to the second. Number 12 was opposite the lift doors.

'What are you going to do?' Tom said.

'Just ring. I'm not sure the porter would have opened it.'

She rang and they could hear the buzzer go just behind the door. She found herself trembling again and held one hand with the other. There was no other sound except music coming from a nearby apartment. She pressed the buzzer again, but the moment the noise died there was silence. Then Tom said, 'There's a TV on.'

They put their ears to the door and Anne could hear low voices and laughter. It sounded like a film. She rang the buzzer again. No one came but the soft voices continued. Frustrated, she tried the door. It opened. She felt Tom's hand gripping her arm as she stepped over the threshold.

It was a medium-sized flat. The front door led into a passageway. Ahead of her was the kitchen and bathroom. To her right was what looked like a larger room.

241

She could see through the half-open door and small dining table and chairs. It was the room from which the noise of the TV was coming.

'Hello!' she said.

There was no answer except the sibilant voices. She moved towards the noise. The room, which was a combined dining room/sitting room was in darkness, lit only by the TV screen. There was a sofa and two soft chairs. On the floor was a plate of potato crisps and an empty glass. The sofa was covered in a pile of blankets and cushions. And then . . . and then in the midst of the pile she could make out a small fair head and a small white hand.

'Hilly!' she cried. 'Oh, Hilly!'

She ran forward and fell to her knees at the sofa. Hilly was lying amid the pillows covered by a blanket. She did not stir as Anne took her in her arms, and for one terrible second, she thought her daughter was dead. Then Hilly groaned in her sleep and Anne held her and suddenly there was a crash of doors and lights came on and the room seemed filled with people. But there were only two: Merrow and Robertson.

'Is she all right?' Merrow asked.

'I think so,' Anne said. 'She's asleep.'

'Thank God for that.'

Hilly groaned again and Tom picked up a small plastic bottle from the dining table. He said, 'She's probably had these. They're an old-fashioned antihistamine that's being marketed as a sleep-inducer.'

'How did you get here?' Merrow said to Anne. She was sitting on the sofa now with the doped child in her arms.

'It's a long story,' she said. 'And you?'

'A woman phoned your house. Your father took the call. She said she had taken an overdose. Gave this address. He phoned Kingstown Central and they got onto us. Both of us happen to live quite close.'

Robertson put his head round the door. 'Come and have a look at this,' he said.

Merrow, followed by Tom with Anne carrying Hilly, went into the bedroom. Stephanie Melville was lying on the bed. She was fully dressed in a black skirt and white blouse just as Miss Garth had remembered. Beside the bed was a half-empty bottle of whisky and an empty plastic container. Tom went to the bed and felt for a pulse.

After a minute or two he said, 'There's nothing. I think she's dead.' His face was ashen.

It was two o'clock in the morning at Anne's house and at last the police had gone. Hilly was in her bed and so was Henry. He and Watch had been at the front door when Anne had carried the child back into the house, and from that moment Watch had not left her. He had taken her out of Anne's arms and carried her upstairs and put her to bed and was even now sitting in her room. He looked a hundred years old, Anne thought, as she went upstairs for the third time to check that Hilly was breathing regularly. When she came down again she realised that they *all* looked a hundred years old.

The hours had gone by slowly. Merrow and Robertson had done their best to make things easy, but there had to be a formal going-through of movements and of why

Tom and Anne had gone to the block of holiday apartments and how they had managed to get in. At first Anne had decided to forget what she had seen in the porter's flat, but when they were telling the two detectives about how they got into the building she thought of all the missing children in England and Europe, and how many of them must be in situations not too dissimilar to the one she had seen that night. So she told Merrow, who took notes and nodded and said he'd 'get into it.' At least she knew she'd done the right thing.

And now they'd gone, and the three of them, Taplin and Tom and Anne, were still in the kitchen. Tom was nursing half a mug of black coffee. He had hardly spoken since he had tried to take Stephanie's pulse. Now he said again what they had all in their own way said before: 'Why? Why did she do it?'

'We'll never know,' Anne said. 'Never.'

But that wasn't good enough for Tom. He shook his head slowly and said, 'You know, she had everything. Looks, money, education, background. Why?'

'You said yourself she wanted things she could never have.'

'Maybe she just wanted to show us how easy it was to lose everything. I think that's what she thought had happened to her. That she'd lost everything. The fact is, once she had something she usually didn't want it. She wanted something else.'

Anne said, 'She wanted sympathy as much as anything else.'

'And she didn't want to die. That's why she phoned. She'd done it all before, and had been found in time.

That's why she left the door of the flat unlocked, so whoever it was could get in.'

Anne said, 'But what she didn't know was that the glass doors would be locked at night.'

'Would it have made any difference?' Taplin said.

Tom shrugged. 'Her body was still warm. It might have. Who knows?'

They had talked about Hilly too, talked and talked, and the common view was that she would have known very little about what had happened. She'd had some crisps, she'd had a drink, and almost certainly with the drink, the antihistamines. She would have known nothing then of Stephanie's death.

In the Land Rover, on the way back from the Santa Rosa, she had briefly come awake, and the first person she had seen was her mother, for Anne was holding her in her arms. She had muttered something. Anne had bent her head and said, 'What did you say, darling?' And Hilly had muttered again: 'Why were you so long?'

That could only have meant one thing: Stephanie had got her there by telling her that Anne was coming. And Anne *had* come. That was the important psychological frame. Tom was certain there would be no resultant trauma. Anne could only hope, but it was a hope tinged with optimism.

They sat tiredly looking at their hands, unable, or unwilling to take the events of the night any further.

Taplin said at last, 'I must be going.'

Anne said, 'I owe you a great deal.'

He shrugged. 'As you said, what if she'd been my little girl.'

'I'll take you home,' Anne told him. Then: 'No, I won't. You take my car. Bring it back when you can.' She went to the door with him and said, 'I won't forget what you did for us and I'll try to make it up to you in any way you like.'

'The only thing I want to do is work. I don't give a damn what sort, just work.'

'I'll do what I can.'

She stood on the pavement and watched the rear lights go down the street and turn at the top. Then there was only darkness.

She went back into the house. Tom said, 'I'm going too.'

'Stay if you like,' Anne said wearily. 'There's a spare bed.'

He shook his head. 'No, I've been neglecting Beanie. Why don't you bring Hilly over to my place tomorrow. It'll take her out of herself.'

She touched his cheek. 'I'll ring you, but it sounds good. And Tom, thank you.'

He kissed his forefinger and touched her lips. 'See you,' he said. She stood at the door for a second time and watched the Land Rover disappear, then she went upstairs to Hilly's room. Watch was still sitting by the bed. His eyes were wide open but he looked more like the old Watch she knew.

'Go to bed,' she said.

'I am not eh-tired,' he said.

'Well, I am.' She touched Hilly's hair then whispered to Watch: 'Good night.'

It was like an ordinary greeting, just as she would have

said any night. Things had become ordinary again. Thank God.

Taplin went into his house, smelling the familiar smell and, tired as he was, felt the surge of pleasure he usually felt; the feeling of pride in ownership.

Then he remembered Ronnie Payne. He looked in the sitting room but there was no figure stretched out on the sofa, and he realised that Ronnie must have gone. He felt relieved. In his exhaustion he had no place for Ronnie right now.

The house was silent. He switched off the sitting room light and the passage light and went to his bedroom. Just before he switched on the light he saw a figure on his bed with a blanket pulled over it. So that's where the bugger had gone. He was in Taplin's own bed and there were two empty beer cans on the floor.

Taplin was too tired to make a fuss. He'd sleep on the sofa for tonight and get rid of Ronnie in the morning. He fetched a blanket from a wall cupboard and went quietly back to the sitting room. He was even too tired to go upstairs and do his teeth. Instead he kicked off his shoes, wrapped the blanket around himself and lay down on the sofa. As he put his head down he heard the soft thud of footsteps above him and sleepily became aware that Betty was still awake. Just before he closed his eyes he remembered that he would have to get Ronnie his breakfast before or after Betty used the kitchen. He didn't particularly want them to meet.

He slept.

It seemed he had only just closed his eyes when he was

woken by a terrible cry. He jerked upright. The cry came again. It was from his bedroom. He ran along the passage clutching the blanket round him. Against the moonlit window he saw a figure standing next to the bed. He switched on the light and the full horror hit him. Betty was standing above Ronnie Payne. She had a long-bladed kitchen knife in her hand, and even as the light came on she drove it down again into Ronnie's body. Blood was spurting up in two rivulets and Payne was holding his chest. He yelled again but that was the last time. He sat up, stared uncomprehendingly at Betty and then his eyes rolled backwards into his head and he fell against the pillows.

Betty turned. She was looking at Taplin with an appalled expression in her eyes and he knew why. The figure in the bed was meant to be him.

'Give me the knife,' he said.

Instead she screamed shrilly and came at him. He had been half-expecting it. He held up the blanket to protect his chest and the knife struck into its folds. He caught her arms. Dragged her towards him. Then he twisted the knife arm now enfolded in the blanket. She screamed again. Then he hit her. He hit her as hard as he could in the face. He felt his knuckles crack. She flew backwards and fell heavily against the bed, sliding onto the floor in a state of unconsciousness.

He was about to use the knife to cut two strips of the blanket to bind her when he abruptly realised that he would be wiping out her fingerprints – and without them, who the hell would believe him? Instead, he ripped up his shirt and bound her arms to the bed leg. Then he went to Ronnie Payne. There were great red holes in his chest. But the blood was no longer pumping from them. Ronnie was dead.

Ivor picked up the phone and dialled 999. A woman's voice said: 'Emergency. Which service?'

'Police,' he said, and then he sat down to wait.